Praise for the Matchmaking Cats of the Goddesses

The humor, chemistry and cattitude in McGraw's books always make them a pleasure to read and this one is no exception. Just when the fated match seems like it is impossible, the cats of the goddesses find a way to make it happen, in spectacular fashion as usual. An absolute must read for paranormal romance fans.

— GOODREADS REVIEWER

Just purr-fect! I laughed so much!

— BOOKBUB REVIEWER

If you love cats and the paranormal, this is the series for you. Meet the magical cats of the goddesses who love matchmaking and getting mates together.

— AMAZON REVIEWER

Matchmaking
Cats
of the
Goddesses

WELCOME to
ZERO, KANSAS
HOME OF
MANY
RESIDENTS

Her Purrfect Familiar

Her Purrfect Familiar

A PAWSITIVELY PURRFECT MATCH

PEPPER MCGRAW

Contents

P
M
G
Publishing

Author's Note

Dear reader,

Welcome to Jo and Annika's story! Their story was quite the challenge to write as it spans the length of multiple other books in this series.

Her Purrfect Familiar begins immediately after *Tridents & Tails* and ends immediately after *Valen-Cats*.

In terms of placement in the series, I've settled *Her Purrfect Familiar* before the matches made in Hell books (*Chocolate Furnanigans, Satan's Kitty, Valen-Cats* and *Catanic Rituals)*, but it can really be read at any point along the way.

Jo's story is also unique in that she met her fated mate back in *Hocus Purrcus* and she and Annika have been living their happily ever after ever since.

This is their story, but it is also a story about the quest for the purrfect familiar for Jo.

In fact, I like to think of *Her Purrfect Familiar* as not only the continuing love story between a witch and her vampiress, but also the love story between that same witch and the cat she's been waiting her entire life to meet.

Now, if only the matchmaking cats of the goddesses can figure out which cat that's supposed to be.

Happy reading!

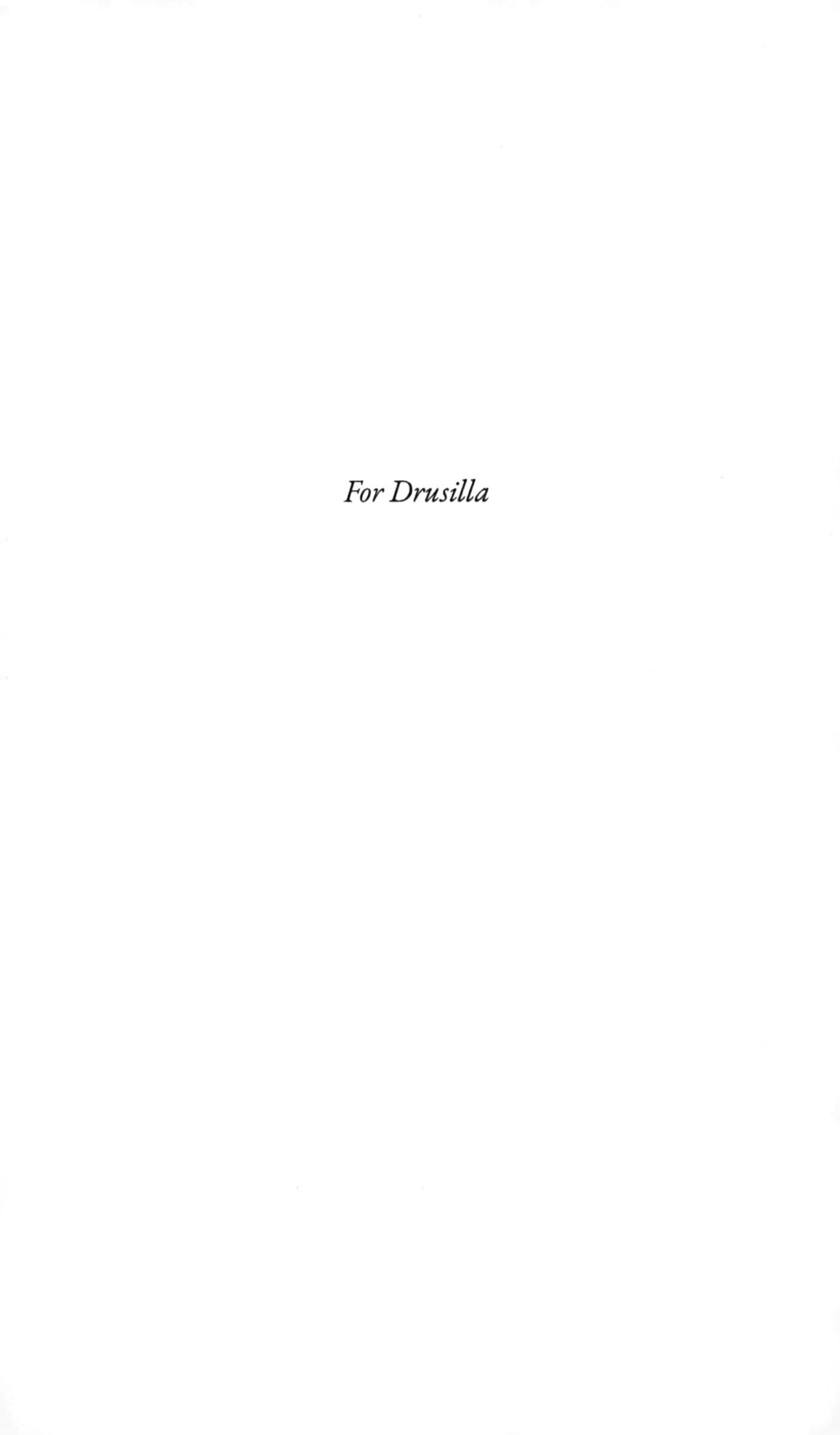

For Drusilla

One

"I *LOVE* MERRY." Soraya was purring so loudly, it was almost impossible to understand her words.

Almost.

Unfortunately, Bygul not only understood them, he knew that Soraya was serious. She really did admire the daughter of Satan.

"You *love* her?" Tivali asked incredulously.

"So much!" Soraya pounced on a blanket and began making biscuits, purring madly all the while.

Bygul was speechless.

Wait.

No, he wasn't.

"Are you mad?" He exclaimed. "Of all the witches in Zero, Kansas, *she's* the one you love?"

"Yep." Soraya leapt away from the blanket, whirled and leapt back onto it, the force carrying both of them several feet.

"She's causing problems left and right," Muezza complained, "and she's not even been here a month!"

"Exactly," Bygul said. "Everywhere we look, it's chaos and it's all because of that witch. How can you possibly love her?"

"Because," Soraya said as she skidded back across the floor in the opposite direction. "She's hilarious."

"She's *not* hilarious," Tivali said sternly. "She's, she's—" Tivali's voice tapered off into a growl, clearly struggling to come up with a suitable description.

"Psycho?" Muezza suggested.

"An aggravating pain in the tail?" Bygul said.

"*Wonderful*," Soraya said.

Tivali twitched her ears in annoyance, then snapped, "Outrageously difficult."

"Oooh, I have a great idea!" Soraya exclaimed.

Highly doubtful. In fact, there was pretty much zero chance this idea would be great by any stretch of the imagination.

Muezza and Tivali clearly agreed because they both let out rumbling growls in Soraya's direction.

Unfortunately, Soraya was having too much fun

playing with that idiotic blanket to pay them any attention. "We should totally match her!"

"Absolutely not," Bygul said. "She's not our target witch."

"Besides," Tivali said. "We all agreed that Jo would be next."

"Exactly," Muezza said. "Jo's waited long enough for her her own familiar. After all, she's the one who ensured a wide pool of mate candidates for the coven."

"Fine," Soraya sighed. She slid to a stop in front of the three of them. "In that case, I suggest Leo."

"Is that the little orange kitten we found on the streets of Chicago last month?" TIvali asked.

"Yep." Soraya twitched her ears in agreement. "He should be purrfect for the garden witch."

Jo skipped down the stairs in her coven's home, a bounce of pure joy in her steps.

The house was quiet now that all thirteen hell-kittens had returned to Hell with Satan.

Even better, the house was gloriously zombie-free since Morana no longer had to raise road kill from the dead as a source of food for the voraciously hungry kittens.

It wouldn't have been so bad except the kittens had been born *inside* the coven house, which meant at any moment, one might encounter zombies wandering through, or worse, witness a hell-kitten attacking and eating said zombies, a sight horrifying enough to give anyone nightmares.

In fact, it was that sight that had made waking in the middle of the night to hell-kittens attacking their toes extra terrifying.

Jo and Annika had taken to wearing multiple pairs of socks and bundling their feet into blankets like little burritos, just to protect them from the murder kittens.

The worst part was that they'd no longer been able to sleep with their legs intertwined. It had simply been too uncomfortable with giant sausage ankles.

They'd still slept in each other's arms, but it hadn't been the same.

Now that the hell-kittens were gone, though, Jo had slept better than ever the night before.

Of course, that might also have to do with the way they'd kissed and indulged their passions long into the night, but they'd had so much to celebrate.

Thirteen hell-kittens were home safe in Hell, and inside the Coven House, no witch, vampire, chameleon or wolf had lost a single toe to the murder kittens—a minor miracle, if you asked Jo.

As Jo and Annika had fallen asleep in each other's arms, legs entwined once more, Jo had vowed to herself that she wasn't going to push their luck any further by continuing to hope for a cat familiar.

She still *wanted* a familiar, of course. Every witch needed one to gain full control of their powers. However, no one said that familiar had to be a cat. Perhaps a bunny familiar would be a better choice.

After all, cats and witches were so *cliche*.

For a reason, of course. Everyone knew that cats were the most powerful and intelligent of all the familiar possibilities, but that didn't mean another familiar wouldn't do.

Besides, there were always exceptions.

Cookie was the perfect example. He wasn't exactly the most intelligent of familiars, despite being a cat.

Jo would feel bad for Tempest, except she also had Kyrie. Cookie was for Tempest's witchy side while Kyrie, the hell-kittens' mom, was for her demonic side, which definitely needed an extra helping of control.

Perhaps Jo would be the first witch with a super-intelligent bunny familiar, who was also a vast source of power.

Hey, it could happen.

"There she is!" Annika cheered as Jo walked into the dining room, where the rest of the coven was eating breakfast. "You were sleeping so soundly, I didn't have to heart to wake you."

Jo immediately changed trajectory from the coffee bar to Annika's side, so that she could pull her mate into her arms and kiss her thoroughly.

Annika responded instantly, leaning into the kiss, fangs tugging at Jo's lips in a move that caused Jo's breath to hitch and stutter.

Jo slowly pulled away, but Annika made a soft sound of protest, prompting Jo to lean in for another kiss as heat barreled through them both.

"Seriously?" Morana exclaimed, her voice seeming to come from a distance. "I'm surrounded by mated witches, while mine continually runs from me. It's just not right."

"Maybe if you'd stop torturing him by raising dead insects whenever he's near," Natalie said.

"Whatever."

Jo chuckled and pulled away from Annika. "To be continued," she murmured against her lips, then kissed her cheek before heading to the coffee bar. "What's everyone up to—" her voice trailed off as she caught sight of the ginger kitten sitting next to the coffee pot.

"Who's this?" she exclaimed, whirling to glare at her coven. "Who got a familiar this time?"

"What are you talking about?" Natalie stood to get

a closer look. "Oh, my goodness, it's a ginger kitty this time."

"He's so cute," Annika exclaimed.

"Guess it's your turn for a familiar, Jo," Rowan said.

"Do you really think so?" Jo stroked the kitten between his ears and giggled when he reared on his hind legs and caught her wrist between his front paws.

She lifted her hand a little and he rose into the air, tail wagging fiercely.

"He's definitely yours," Pippa said.

"Besides, every single one of us walked by that countertop this morning and he didn't appear for any of us," Natalie said. "Clearly, he's here for you."

"Come here, baby." Jo scooped the kitten into her arms and about melted when he turned his attention to the ties on her hoodie and began batting them fiercely.

"Look, Annika." Jo turned and beamed at her mate. "Isn't he adorable?"

"So cute," Annika agreed.

"What are you going to name him?" Tempest asked.

"I don't know." Jo walked to the table and settled in the chair to the right of Annika. "I have to get to know him first, so for now, he can just be my little buttercup. Isn't that right, sweet buttercup?" She set him on the table and everyone watched as he pounced on a napkin, fell onto his side and began to wrestle the napkin into submission.

"I hate to admit it," Natalie's mate, Corwin, said, "but that kitten is freaking adorable."

This was high praise coming from the wolf. He was right, of course.

"I'm so in love right now," Jo announced.

"Should I be jealous?" Annika asked with a grin.

Jo snickered. "Maybe." She winked at Annika. Then, because she could never resist her mate's allure for long, she leaned over and kissed her until they were both breathless. "Then again, no familiar could possibly hold a candle to you, my love."

"Oh, gag me," Rowan muttered.

Annika giggled and Jo grinned. "Don't worry, Rowan. I'm sure my spell will bring your mate to you soon."

He growled. "Not helpful, Jo."

"Yeah, not helpful. At all." Morana scowled. "Your spell brought my mate to me and he runs every time he sees me, so frankly, Jo, I would have preferred you cast a spell for our familiars, rather than our fated mates."

"I didn't have to since the familiars appear to be showing up of their own accord. Aren't they, my sweet little Buttercup? You're the best kitten ever. Yes, you are!"

"I'm a genius," Soraya announced.

"Does anyone else think that was just a little too easy?" Muezza asked.

"Of course it was easy," Tivali said. "The hard part is matching the humans to their mates. Jo already found hers, so all we had to do was get her to fall in love with a cat. I bet any cat would have made her happy."

"Yes, but happy isn't the only goal, at least not with the witches," Bygul said. "The cats aren't just companions. They're familiars. They have to help the witches come into their full power *and* gain control of their magic. We may think this was an easy match, but we still have to keep an eye on the situation, just to make sure it turns into a pawsitively purrfect one."

"Oh, it will be," Soraya insisted. "I have a sense about these things. Buttercup and Jo are going to be so happy together."

"No, no, no!" Jo exclaimed as Buttercup raced through her garden, attacking vines that slithered along the ground and climbed trellises.

She ran after him, but was too late to stop him from launching to the top of a trellis, where he proceeded to wrestle one of her tomato plants into submission.

Jo sent one of the vines to scoop him off the trellis and deposit him into her arms.

Buttercup did *not* like that development at all.

Fur standing on end, he spat and swatted at the vine as it retreated from them.

"It's okay, Buttercup, it's okay," Jo crooned. "The vines aren't going to hurt you, I promise." She sighed. "Let's go visit the flower garden instead, shall we?"

Cuddling Buttercup close, she hurried through the vegetable garden, trying to convince herself that this wasn't a deal-breaker. Surely the cat could be trained.

"I may have made a tiny miscalculation," Soraya admitted as Buttercup raced through the flower garden, attacking pansies and marigolds and rolling in a bed of snapdragons.

"You think?" Muezza said dryly as Buttercup

decapitated three daisies and began chasing their petals all through the garden.

When they'd first arrived in the flower garden, Jo had tried to control the kitten, but she appeared to have given up and now simply stood, a look of dazed shock on her face.

"Well, to be honest, he wasn't my first choice for Jo."

"What?" Bygul exploded. "You can't just choose a substitute, Soraya. You have to listen to your instincts. What were they telling you?"

"There's this cat on Kalyn's caseload."

"Oh, no. No, no, no," Bygul said. "We are *not* stealing one of Kalyn's cats. He'll never let me hear the end of it."

"Oh, he already offered this cat to everyone. No one wants to take him."

"So why haven't *I* heard about this cat then?" Bygul said.

"Okay, so maybe not *everyone*," Soraya said, "but he offered him to me."

"And me," Tivali admitted.

"Me too," Muezza said.

"Why is Kalyn so determined to get rid of this cat?"

"He's kind of—well, grumpy."

"Cleocatra grumpy or Shredder grumpy?"

Soraya thought about that a moment, then decided, "Poseidon grumpy."

"Seriously?" Bygul exclaimed. "Why would you want to match that level of grumpiness with Jo? She's so happy all that time."

"I don't know. They just seemed like the purrfect match."

"Well, we can't try Grumpy Cat until we figure out what to do with Leo Buttercup over there," Tivali said. "We can't just leave him with the garden witch. He'll drive her mad within a day."

"Any ideas?" Bygul asked.

"I don't think we'll have to do anything," Muezza said. "Sounds like the garden witch already has a plan."

JO PACED BACK AND FORTH, BUTTERCUP riding her shoulder, playing with her hair as she explained to her Coven everything that had happened in the garden.

"I'm a green witch," Jo wailed. "I can't have a familiar who thinks my plants are his own personal chew toys!"

"Sounds more like he was treating them like wand toys," Rowan observed.

"Except for the cherry tomatoes," Morana said. "He was chasing those, right?"

"I think he's adorable," Merry announced. "He's the color of flames! If you really don't want him, Jo, he'd make the purrfect gift for Aunt Lucinda."

"Don't you dare," Tempest growled. "Lucinda has no need for a kitten and especially not a mortal one. If you want to give her a kitten, talk to Dad. He has plenty of hell-kittens to spare."

"Hm. Now there's an idea."

"We should give him to Lucky," Natalie announced.

"Say what now?" Matthew looked appalled.

"That's a great idea!" Tempest exclaimed.

"You're crazy," Matthew said.

"But Lucky loves cats," Tempest said. "Surely you've noticed how happy she is whenever we show up at the diner with our familiars."

"Yes, but Lucky's mated to Darren, which means she lives with the Coalition," Matthew said. "There's a reason we never bring the cats when visiting the other chameleons."

"You're just a pessimist today." Tempest whirled to face Jo. "I think this is the best idea ever. Besides, imagine the benefits of having a leprechaun named Lucky owing the Coven a favor."

"I've never placed a cat with a Coalition before," Bygul said. "Now I'm curious why the chameleon thinks it's a bad idea. What's wrong with chameleons?"

"You mean besides confusing everyone about who and what they are?" Tivali asked.

"And besides being expert con artists?" Muezza asked.

"Okay, but it's not like they're going to try and con earthbound cats, so what's so scary about letting them visit the Coalition?" Bygul asked.

"Maybe chameleon magic works on earthbound cats like it does on humans," Tivali suggested.

"I think we're about to find out," Soraya said. "Matthew just called Lucky and it sounds like she and Darren are on their way right now to pick up Leo Buttercup. Isn't this exciting? We're going to match two cats on this one! I love it when that happens."

"He's so cute," Lucky squealed, scooping Buttercup into her hands.

Jo tried not to show how devastated she was to have had a familiar for less than a day. She'd considered keeping the kitten anyway, but everywhere she went, plants grew and flowers blossomed.

Her bedroom was covered in foliage and she couldn't imagine the amount of energy it would take to constantly monitor the kitten and keep it from attacking everything she grew.

"I'm so depressed," Jo confessed to Annika as they lay in bed together that night.

"Don't be sad, Jo," Annika murmured, laying kisses along her jawline and nuzzling into her hair. "Little Buttercup found the perfect home for him and that's because of you and your generosity. You didn't hold onto him, even though you already loved him, because you knew someone else would be a better fit. Just like there's another familiar out there, who will be the perfect fit for you. I'm absolutely sure of it. You just have to be patient and have faith."

"Oh, Annika, I'm so blessed, to have you for my mate." Jo rolled them so that she was on top, then leaned down and kissed Annika, murmuring against her lips, "If I never get another chance for a familiar, that'll be okay because you are truly everything that I need."

Annika slid her hands through Jo's hair and tilted her head up so their eyes met. "Just don't give up, okay? You're everything to me too, which is why *I'm* not giving up. I truly *believe* your familiar will come to you in time." She pulled Annika down for another blazing hot kiss, one that sent ripples of heat rolling through them both.

Silence fell in the bedroom as the passion and love that had gripped them from the moment they met consumed them in a rush of ecstasy and fire.

"YOU KNOW, DARLING," Darren said as they walked into the Coalition Compound, "I'm not sure having a cat inside the Coalition is a good idea."

"It's a perfect idea," Lucky protested. "He's so sweet and we don't have any pets. I was thinking we should adopt an entire colony of cats. That would be so awesome, don't you think?"

Darren blanched. "I think that's maybe optimistic. Let's see how the kitten does and we'll go from there. What are you going to call him?"

Lucky gasped. "He's Buttercup, of course. I can't just change his name, as if the one he has doesn't count or something."

Darren rolled his eyes. "I'm pretty sure he'd be thrilled if you'd change that stupid name."

"Don't listen to him, Buttercup," Lucky said. "You have an absolutely marvelous name."

"You do realize buttercups are toxic to cats, right?" Darren asked.

"What are you talking about?"

"Buttercups. They're flowers and they're toxic to cats. You'd think a witch who specializes in growing things would know that."

"Maybe she just liked the dichotomy of the name."

"See, Bygul?" Soraya said. "There's nothing scary here. The kitten's doing just fine."

"You brought a kitten to the compound, Darren?" a chameleon exclaimed as they walked into the main dining room where members of the Coalition were eating dinner.

"That doesn't sound fine to me," Bygul said ominously.

"Meow." Buttercup leapt from Lucky's arms, landed on a table and began to strut down it, pausing to meow at every chameleon along the way.

"What's he doing?" Tivali asked.

"Greeting the other cats, of course," Soraya said.

"What other—oh. Huh. I didn't notice them before. How strange." Tivali shook her head and looked around the room. "Where are all the chameleons? Are all these cats just living here by themselves?"

"I've never seen a colony this big before," Muezza observed.

"Does this mean we need to add them to our case-load too?" Soraya asked.

"Well, we do have a duty to ensure the cats we encounter are all happy. If they're cared for and happy here, we don't necessarily have to add them to our case-load, but we do need to make sure," Bygul said.

"Look at that," Soraya said. "Buttercup's already making so many friends."

They all watched as the other cats greeted the kitten, bumping heads with him, rubbing up against him and accepting him into their midst.

"Ah," Tivali said. "I just *love* a happy ending."

"It's not a happy ending until we're sure all the cats are happy here," Bygul said. "Spread out and start taking notes, matchmakers. Any cats who seem unhealthy, too thin *or* lethargic will need immediate placement elsewhere."

Soraya was trying to decide if one cat was just a

loner and happy to be alone, or if he was in pain, when Nefertiti showed up.

"What in all the Realms are you *doing,* Soraya?" Nefertiti demanded.

"Nefertiti!" Soraya exclaimed excitedly. "I'm so happy to see you. We discovered this entire colony of cats and we're trying to decide who needs a new placement. Mostly the cats seem purrfectly happy and healthy, but this one." She shook her head and stared hard at the large cat eating all by himself. "He seems a bit lonely. Sad, really."

"Don't be ridiculous, Soraya," Nefertiti exclaimed. "That is *not* a cat! That is a chameleon and you have fallen prey to the most potent of demonic magic. You have access to the magic of the goddesses, for Egypt's sake. Now look at him again, this time with clear eyes."

Soraya felt a little strange, like the world was covered in a layer of glass that shimmered for a moment before stabilizing.

That was when she realized the "cat" she'd been examining was actually a chameleon. A rather large chameleon who seemed most intent on eating his food and ignoring all the other chameleons in the room, who were busy charming the kitten in their midst.

"Oh, my goddess," Soraya breathed. "I thought we were immune to chameleon magic."

"Well, sure, when confronting one or two, but not when you're dumb enough to waltz right into an entire compound full of the creatures! You're a matchmaking cat of the goddesses, Soraya, not a goddess herself. Now let's get your foolish companions and get out of here. I've come to visit my sweetie-pie, to assure myself that he's doing well in the Earth realm. He is, isn't he?"

"Wait until you see him, Nefertiti. Cookie is so happy with Tempest, you wouldn't believe it. He'll be thrilled you visited though." Chatting happily, Soraya led Nefertiti across the room to collect Tivali, then Muezza and finally, Bygul, who was quite annoyed when he realized that he, too, had fallen prey to the magic of the Coalition.

TEMPEST AND MATTHEW WERE HALFWAY UP the stairs, following Kyrie and Cookie as they led the way toward their bedroom, when Cookie suddenly slid to a stop, whirled and barreled back down the stairs, hurtling by faster than Tempest had ever seen him move before.

A moment later, the Coven door blew open and a

woman's voice called, "Sweetie-pie, come here, my sweet baby!"

Kyrie, who had made it halfway down the hall by that point, let out a growl and barreled back toward them.

She grew to her largest form in a fraction of a second and cleared the entire staircase in one bound, skidding to a halt in the front room, fur bristling, growling at the very exotic-looking woman standing there.

A woman who was currently cuddling Cookie in her arms.

Cookie looked as content as Tempest had ever seen him, stretched out in her arms, a blissful look on his face, purrs rumbling from his throat.

Who in all the Realms of Hell was this woman and what was she doing with *Tempest's* familiar?

Tempest let out a growl of her own and stamped down the stairs, keenly aware that Matthew was following silently while the rest of her Coven slid into position all along the staircase, ready to provide back-up if necessary.

"Can I help you?" Tempest snarled. She might have tried to say it nicely, but, well, the woman was cuddling *her* cat.

And Cookie was enjoying it!

Rude!

"UNBELIEVABLE," BYGUL MUTTERED. "WE spend all this time making sure the humans never see us and here comes Nefertiti, prancing around in all her goddess-like, former queen-of-Egypt glory."

"Hello, dear," Nefertiti said to Tempest, who looked irritated, if Bygul was any judge of human emotions. And he *was,* which meant he was actually understating the case because in truth, Tempest looked pawsitively *murderous.*

"Um, maybe you should give the demoness her cat, Nefertiti," Soraya said nervously.

"Demoness? *Really?*" Nefertiti stared at Tempest closely. "Oh, my. And not just *any* demoness. I'm impressed. You've outdone yourself with this match, Soraya. If anyone can ensure my sweetie-pie is safe and well cared for, it would certainly be a daughter of Satan."

Kyrie stalked closer, letting out an even louder growl than before.

"Oh, my!" Nefertiti gave a tiny hop of excitement. "And a hell-cat. I haven't seen one of those in so very long."

Dear goddess, Bygul now understood exactly where Soraya got her enthusiasm. It was all the queen of Egypt's fault.

From now on, every time Soraya got them into a crazy situation, he was going to blame her *and* Nefertiti.

The chameleon edged closer to his mate and muttered in her ear, "Uh, who's she talking to, Tempest?"

Tempest just glared at the woman. "What are you doing here, Nefertiti, and *why* are you cuddling my cat?"

"*Nefertiti?*" The chameleon exclaimed. "As in the queen of Egypt, Nefertiti? This is a joke, right?"

"Oh, what a wondrous afterlife this is, indeed! I'm so flattered you recognize me." Nefertiti let out a tinkling giggle, then stepped forward and carefully passed Cookie to Tempest.

The demoness, Bygul noticed, looked relieved and significantly less murderous now that Cookie was safe in her arms.

The hell-cat also stopped growling quite so loudly.

Cookie let out a plaintive meow and Nefertiti chuckled. "Of course, I'll visit again, sweetie-pie. It was simply marvelous to see you, but I'm afraid I must go now. A queen of Egypt never rests, you know, not even in the afterlife." Nefertiti touched the fingers of both hands to her lips, then blew a kiss to Kyrie with her left hand and settled the fingers of her right on Cookie's head. "Be good, my love," she murmured to him, then disappeared.

"I'm sorry," Matthew said into the silence that followed. "She was Nefertiti? *The* Nefertiti, Queen of Egypt, dead for more than three thousand years, *that* Nefertiti?"

"It's okay, Matthew," Tempest said. "If you don't think about it too much, by tomorrow, you'll be convinced she was just an ordinary woman. That's the way goddess magic works. Come along, now, I think it's time for bed." Carrying Cookie in her arms, she led the way up the stairs, Matthew and Kyrie following silently.

The rest of the coven stood frozen on the stairs as she passed them by, not one of them looking as if they'd avoid thinking about what had just happened, Bygul couldn't help but notice.

"So!" Soraya spoke brightly. "Shall we go see if Grumpy Cat's ready to meet Jo?"

The answer, they discovered a few minutes later, was *no.*

Grumpy Cat glared and refused to move when Soraya attempted to coax him into coming with them.

Bygul had never seen a more uncooperative cat in his life and that was saying something, considering the many cats he'd matched through the years.

"Here's what I think," Bygul finally said when he got tired of listening to Soraya attempt to sweet-talk the stubborn cat. "Your instincts are clearly on the fritz, Soraya. First, you choose the plant-eater for the garden witch, then you get us all trapped at the Coalition, *then* Nefertiti shows up!"

"You can't blame me for that," Soraya protested.

"Of course, I can," Bygul said. "You're the one who took Cookie to the afterlife and left him with Nefertiti in the first place. If you'd taken him to the waiting room, Nefertiti would never have met him, so yes, I do blame you."

"How rude!" Soraya exclaimed with an impertinent twitch of her tail.

Bygul ignored her and turned to the sensible cat of their group. "Tivali, who would *you* choose for Jo?"

Tivali looked uncertain, which wasn't a good sign, but she finally said, "The calico over there. She's very sweet, like Jo. She should be a purrfect match for the garden witch."

After all the excitement the night before, Jo and Annika slept late.

They'd stayed up, discussing Nefertiti with the rest of the Coven. "A queen of Egypt visited us," Morana kept saying in awe.

Everyone agreed that if she visited again, they would be sure to introduce themselves and ask her questions about the afterlife. After all, she'd looked pretty damn good for a dead woman.

It was because she was exhausted from the late night that Jo first thought she was hallucinating when she came out of the bathroom upstairs and found a calico cat waiting for her in the hallway.

Jo glanced up and down the hall, but no one else seemed to be around. "What are you doing here, huh? How'd you get in, anyway?"

Of course, the cat had no answer. She just let out a small, dainty meow, then launched herself into Jo's arms.

Jo stumbled back in surprise, then giggled. "Well, aren't you the sweetest thing?" She rubbed noses with the cat, then settled her against her shoulder and sauntered down the stairs.

As she moved toward the dining room and heard the sounds of her Coven eating breakfast, she had a visceral feeling of deja vu, but then she heard Merry's voice.

She had no idea where Merry had been the day before, but she'd been rather grateful to not have the *other* daughter of Satan hanging around, witnessing her difficulties with Buttercup.

"Hopefully today will be a much better day," she said to the kitten, "especially now that we've got *two* demonesses in the house."

"Anyone missing a cat?" Jo asked as she entered the dining room.

"You found another kitty!" Annika squealed, jumping up to race around the table. "Where'd you find her?" She scratched the cat's head and received a rumbling purr in response.

"She was upstairs, waiting outside the bathroom for me," Jo said.

"Well, that's proof enough for me," Natalie said. "Congratulations, Jo, the goddesses must really like you, to have sent a second candidate so quickly after the first."

Jo would have rolled her eyes at that statement, except they'd been visited by a literal queen of Egypt just the day before, so she figured she should probably keep an open mind.

"What are you going to name this one?" Morana asked.

"I'm not sure," Jo said as she and Annika settled at the table.

The moment they were seated, the calico leapt from Jo's arms onto the table, then sat right between Annika and Jo on the very edge of the table, tail swinging between them, spine straight, a regal look on her face as she examined each of the other coven members sitting at the table.

"She reminds me of someone right now," Tempest said. "I can't quite picture who."

"Nefertiti," Rowan said decisively. "She's Nefertiti from the top of her head to the tip of her tail."

Jo stared at the calico and had to admit that Rowan was right. Despite being a cat, the calico sat like a queen and the look on her face was *pure* Nefertiti. "Normally, I'd wait a while, get to know the cat before assigning a name, but in this case, I think you're right," Jo said, "so I'm going to name her Neferkitty."

"Wait until I tell Nefertiti this," Soraya chortled. "She'll be so flattered."

"Doubtful," Bygul said. "Remember Cleopatra's reaction?"

"That's because she's a drama queen," Soraya said.

"And Nefertiti isn't?" Tivali exclaimed.

"Fine. I guess I won't tell her."

"Probably for the best," Muezza said.

Bygul agreed wholeheartedly. The queens of Egypt could be so damn melodramatic.

"We've done it again, team," Soraya exclaimed. "Jo and Neferkitty are a purrfect match. Nothing could possibly pull them apart now."

The other three cats groaned.

"What?"

"Why would you say that?" Bygul demanded.

"You just tempted the fates," Tivali snapped. "*Again.*"

"I did not. I was just celebrating, like we always do."

"Celebrating is one thing," Muezza said. "Issuing a challenge to the fates is definitely another."

"I didn't challenge them!"

"WHO WANTS A DRINK?" MERRY ASKED AS SHE got up from the table.

"It's ten o'clock in the morning," Tempest said. "A little early for drinks, don't you think?"

"It's midnight somewhere," Merry said. "Besides, I didn't mean alcohol, though we do need to celebrate Jo finding a new familiar." She sauntered into the kitchen and returned a few moments later with a two-liter bottle in hand. "I have it on good authority that Dr. Pepper is the best this realm has to offer in terms of drinks."

"Whose authority would that be?" Jared asked dryly.

"Tiktok," Merry said cheerfully as she twisted the lid off the bottle, which resulted in soda exploding from the top and pouring down the sides. "Wow! That seems an extreme reaction." She held the bottle away from her body and eyed it warily. "I didn't expect it to be so sticky."

She wandered back into the kitchen, where they heard water running. A few moments later, she returned with a tray full of glasses in one hand and the bottle of Dr. Pepper in the other. "Who wants to try it?"

Jo happened to love Dr. Pepper, as did Annika, so she quickly claimed a glass for each of them.

Once everyone had a drink, whatever their chosen drink was, Merry lifted her glass. "To Jo's new familiar, Neferkitty, may they be a match made in Hell."

Jo, who had just taken a sip of her Dr. Pepper, spewed it across the table in a coughing fit.

Rowan snorted with laughter while Tempest leaned over to assure both Jo and Annika that, "She meant it as a good thing. Matches made in Hell are highly coveted."

"In what world?" Matthew snorted.

"In the Nine Realms of Hell, of course," Tempest snapped back.

"I like this drink, this Dr. Pepper," Merry announced. "It's potent. It makes all kinds of things bubble inside. It burns, but not. It's like fire, but not." She took another gulp. "Are we certain this is an earth drink? Seems like it should have been made in the fires of Hell, it's just that good." She guzzled the last drops from her glass, then reached for the bottle to pour some more. "We're going to need more of this nectar from the demons."

"You know, maybe you should slow down," Tempest said, looking a bit worried.

"Slow down? Why in all the Realms would I do that?" Merry asked.

"Have you ever tried soda before?" Annika asked. "It can have unexpected side effects."

"Really? Like what?" Merry guzzled the next glass as quickly as she had the first.

"Heartburn, indigestion, belching," Rowan said.

"Heartburn," Merry repeated. "Does that mean your heart catches fire? Because if so, don't worry, I'm a demoness. Partly anyway. Fire doesn't hurt me."

"Well, your heart doesn't literally *burn,*" Jo explained. "It just feels like it."

"Interesting. So far, no burning. Maybe I need some more." She got up and headed for the kitchen.

"This is going to be bad," Tempest said. "I just know it. She doesn't handle pain well."

"Who does?" Morana asked.

"Yes, but none of you turn into a raving lunatic when the pain gets to be too much."

"This stuff is amazing," Merry declared as she walked back into the dining room, a third bottle with its top already off in her hand. This time, she didn't bother with a glass.

She simply tilted her head back and poured the Dr. Pepper down her throat in one endless drink.

"How is she not drowning?" Annika asked.

"How is she breathing?" Amaryllis whispered.

Jo couldn't take her eyes away from the horror show that was Merry consuming an entire two-liter bottle of soda in one giant swallow.

"I'm finally getting it," Morana muttered. "She's really not human at all."

"Not even a little bit," Tempest agreed.

"Ahhh." Merry let out a sound of satisfaction so potent, Jo had the fleeting thought that soda companies could hire her to do all their advertising. All she'd need to do was drink and sigh and they'd all hire her on the spot.

Then, Merry opened her mouth and let loose the loudest, roaring belch Jo had ever heard. It went on forever and with it came the fires of Hell.

Flames spewed across the dining room table catching everyone's food on fire.

Neferkitty let out a yowl of alarm and barreled into Jo's arms.

Everyone leapt back from the table and watched as the fire raged, the echo of Merry's belch still ringing in their ears.

Kyrie raced into the room, Cookie on her heels, and leapt for the table. The minute her paws hit its surface, the flames all sizzled out.

A moment later, the dining room table crumbled to ash.

"Great!" Tempest exclaimed. "That's the third dining room table this year." She glared at her sister, then at Pippa, who just grinned and shrugged.

"Mrawr!" Neferkitty yowled and leapt from Jo's arms onto Kyrie, who let out a yowl of her own.

Neferkitty sank her teeth into Kyrie's ear and scratched at the back of her head as if the hell-cat was a chew toy.

"Rawr, rawr, rawr!" Kyrie yowled and took off running, Neferkitty clinging to her neck, clearly trying her best to tear the hell-cat's ear off.

"Kyrie, no!" Tempest shouted at the same time Jo wailed, "Neferkitty, no!"

"What do I always say when we make these matches?" Bygul whirled and glared at Soraya.

She sighed. "Never tempt the fates."

"Exactly! Now look at this disaster and all because you had to go and tempt them anyway!"

"You're so dramatic," Soraya said. "I'm sure we'll find the purrfect familiar for Jo soon enough. I was thinking, though."

The other three cats groaned.

"Not again, Soraya," Muezza said.

"Yes, again. I really, *really* think we should match Merry."

"No!" The other three shouted.

"But it'll be fun!"

"*Fun?*" Tivali exclaimed.

"Are you *crazy?*" Bygul exploded.

"What?" Soraya said innocently. "I thought you guys would enjoy the challenge."

"We're focusing on Jo and that's the end of it," Bygul said.

"Fine. But I want it noted that I'm voting for Merry next."

"Not. Happening," Bygul growled.

Three

IT TOOK THE entire coven to corner the hell-cat and a lot of crooning and soft-spoken promises before Jo managed to coax Neferkitty into letting Kyrie's ear go.

Jo then held a trembling Neferkitty in her arms until she finally settled down.

Tempest had to take Kyrie out of the house entirely because Neferkitty wouldn't settle as long as she could sense the hell-cat.

"What set her off?" Merry asked.

"The fire definitely," Jo said, "but then I think the fact that Kyrie made it stop and some of the flames sort of sank into her skin *really* freaked Neferkitty out."

"That's a definite problem," Natalie observed.

"Kyrie's in the house all the time. There's no way we'll be able to keep the two cats apart."

"Maybe she'll adjust," Jo said.

"Maybe," Natalie said doubtfully.

She didn't adjust.

The minute Tempest walked back into Coven House with Kyrie, Neferkitty started to yowl and hiss and spit at the hell-cat.

Then, to make matter worse, Merry wandered through with another two-liter in her hand and set the drapes on fire before wandering out again.

Kyrie sucked down the flames once more and Neferkitty went nuts.

It took Jo and Annika together to keep hold of the kitten while they raced upstairs to their room and shut themselves inside.

They sat on the bed, Jo with her head in Annika's lap, and watched as Neferkitty stalked around the room, exploring every corner and yowling her distress.

"I'm going to have to give her away too," Jo said. "It's not fair, Annika."

"I'm so sorry, my love." Annika stroked Jo's head, sifting her fingers through her hair and scratching her scalp gently. "We'll find her a happy home, somewhere we can visit her as often as we like, until your perfect familiar finally arrives."

"Do you think your coven would take her in?" Jo asked.

"The vampires?" Annika exclaimed incredulously.

"On account of them hating fire."

Annika snickered.

Jo turned her head to stare up into Annika's face, realizing she'd never actually asked about this particular aspect of vampire lore. She knew they had fangs and enjoyed the taste of blood, but that they also ate food just like every other living creature.

She knew sunlight didn't make them burst into flames, but they did avoid the sun on account of the terrible burns. Now, based on Annika's reaction, she assumed the fire thing was probably another myth humans had gotten wrong. "Or not?"

"Definitely not." Annika grinned and dropped a quick kiss on her lips. "I mean, vampires used to live in the Hell realm, for goddess' sake, so it's not like we weren't around fires and the flames of Hell for most of our existence. I suppose some of us probably don't *like* fire, but no more than any other life form. I mean, it's fire. If you're not careful with it, you might burn things you love. Not us, though. We wouldn't burn or anything."

"Right." Jo giggled. "Still, if we give Neferkitty to your coven, we could visit her whenever we want. I should have thought to send Buttercup to them instead of the Chameleons. No one ever gets invited to visit them, not unless you're mated into the Coalition."

"I suppose. I'll have to think about which vampire would be best suited to Neferkitty, but we'll take her to them tomorrow." Annika raised her voice at the end to be heard over Neferkitty's yowling. "Or maybe we should take her today."

Neferkitty yowled even louder.

"Or now. Maybe now. What do you think?"

"Definitely now," Jo agreed.

When they reached the main floor and announced where they were going, Morana immediately offered to drive.

By the time they made it out of the house and to Morana's truck, Amaryllis and Rowan had joined them.

"Just along for the ride," Rowan said as he climbed into the front passenger seat.

"And for moral support," Amaryllis whispered as she joined Jo and Annika in the back.

"I think you should give Neferkitty to Blade," Morana announced once they were on their way.

"Of course, you do," Jo said with a sigh. Blade was

the vampire Morana was shamelessly pursuing, despite the fact that he was terrified of her.

By the time they arrived at the Vampire Coven House, Morana had somehow managed to convince Jo to let her do all the talking.

Mostly, Jo agreed because she knew whatever came out of Morana's mouth was bound to be entertaining in the extreme.

Besides, this was perhaps the only opportunity Morana would have to corner Blade and *not* have him run away from her.

Jo had a terrible time restraining her laugh when they arrived and Blade greeted Morana's offer of a cat with grave suspicion. "Is it a zombie cat?"

"Of course not," Morana exclaimed.

"I don't know why you said it like *that*," Blade said, "as if a zombie cat's outside the realm of possibility. Whenever you're involved, I imagine anything's likelier to be a zombie than not."

"Rude," Morana said, "and in this case, not true. The cat is very much alive and needs a home. Would you like to meet her or not?"

"I suppose, but if she tries to eat my brains, I'll never trust you again."

"So damn melodramatic," Morana muttered as Jo unzipped the carrier and lifted out Neferkitty.

"Oh, she's *gorgeous*!" Blade happily accepted Neferkitty into his arms and immediately began crooning soft words of nonsense to her. "Aren't you the most precious thing ever?" He wandered away, lavishing adoration all over the cat and completely ignoring Morana, who looked quite put out at the vampire's lack of attention.

"I guess we can go then." Morana let out a huff of exasperation.

Before any of them could respond, though, Lassiter came rushing up, clearly thrilled that Amaryllis was inside his territory. He immediately offered them a tour, sweeping Amari under his arm and leading the way inside the vampire coven house.

The tour lasted so long, they ended up staying for dinner, giving Jo, Annika and Rowan front-row seats to the ridiculous courtship of Blade by Morana and the sweet one of Amaryllis by Lassiter.

"You do realize both those romances are doomed, right?" Jo whispered to Annika, who appeared completely charmed by the romance of it all.

"Of course they're not doomed," she whispered back. "They're fated mates. You know they are!"

"I sincerely hope you're wrong because if they *are* fated mates, it's my fault they found each other, and I've never seen four people less suited for each other.

Look at them! Amaryllis is so shy, she barely speaks over a whisper, even with us, and Lassiter is the king of vampires for goddess' sake!"

"But he's so careful with her, so charming," Annika protested.

"She's right," Rowan said. "Plus, have you seen the way Amari looks at him when she thinks he's not watching? She's totally enamored."

Jo rolled her eyes. "Okay, maybe those two will make it. *Maybe.* But Morana and Blade? He's terrified of her!"

"Yeah, but sometimes terror can be exciting," Annika said.

Jo scoffed and Rowan snickered.

"No, seriously. There's a reason horror movies are so popular."

"If you say so," Jo said.

"Uh, Lassiter," a vampire Jo hadn't met yet appeared at Lassiter's side. "There's apparently a fire at Library Zero. Someone mentioned the flames of Hell."

"I can't believe you think Merry's wonderful, Soraya," Tivali said sourly.

"She is!" Soraya exclaimed.

"She's a fire-belching pain in the tail, that's what she is," Bygul said.

"She had the fire out by the time the vampires got there," Soraya said. "She even managed to keep the humans from noticing. Not even the librarian realized something was wrong. That's pretty fast thinking, if you asked me."

"I can't imagine why she was even in the library in the first place," Muezza said. "It seems the least likely place one might find a daughter of Satan."

"She's definitely up to something," Tivali said. "I saw her at the diner the other day, chatting with a little girl. A *human* girl."

"That must be Starlight's daughter," Soraya said.

"Who?" Bygul asked.

"Starlight. The human waitress. They had lunch together last week. Merry was telling Starlight all about her father, even shared a picture and everything."

"She what?" The other three exclaimed.

Soraya reared back with a tiny hiss, startled at their enthusiasm. *"What?"*

"Her dad's Satan!" Bygul exploded.

"Well, she didn't mention that part. They were just talking, that's all."

"Why would she show a picture of Satan to a human?" Bygul demanded.

"I told you. She's up to something," Tivali said.

"Great," Bygul muttered.

"I'm sure that conversation was purrfectly innocent," Soraya said.

Muezza let out a snort of disbelief.

"Anyway, I was thinking," Soraya said, prompting the other cats to groan.

"Not again, Soraya," Tivali said.

"Hey!" Soraya let out a meow of annoyance.

"Let's hear it," Bygul sighed.

"Since you haven't been willing to consider matching Merry, I was thinking maybe our next match could be the librarian instead. Her name's Jane."

"No!" The other cats exclaimed in unison.

Soraya jumped and snarled in surprise. "Rude."

"We need to focus on Jo," Bygul said.

"I know that. It's why I said our *next* match. *After* Jo."

"After Jo, we're choosing another witch and that's final," Bygul said.

Soraya let out a growl, then said, "Fine. Let's go choose another cat for Jo then."

"Cheer up, Soraya," Tivali said right before they popped into the waiting room. "Maybe Grumpy Cat will be ready this time."

He *wasn't*.

In fact, when Soraya tried to get him to play with her, he responded with a hiss and a swat of the paw.

"Well, how rude," Soraya said. "Fine. We'll choose a different cat. Again."

This time Muezza chose a sleek, black cat. "It's truly depressing how many black cats and kittens we have on our caseload," Muezza grumbled as they left the waiting room.

"On all our caseloads," Soraya agreed. "It doesn't make sense, but then humans rarely do."

"Apparently, they believe black cats are unlucky," Tivali said.

"That's ridiculous," Bygul grumbled. "Color has nothing to do with luck. *Luck* has nothing to do with luck. It's just random, that's all."

"You know what's worse than having so many black cats on our caseload?" Soraya asked.

"What's that?" Tivali asked.

"Having a mean, grumpy *almost*-black cat on *everybody's* caseload. No one wants him. It breaks my heart." As they traveled back to the coven house, Soraya pondered the issue of black cats and kittens and an almost-black, very grumpy cat, and was struck with a bit of genius inspiration.

It was a truly marvelous idea, but first, they had to deliver the third candidate to Jo.

JO WASN'T EVEN A LITTLE SURPRISED WHEN she woke the next morning to a black cat sitting at the end of her bed.

Clearly the universe was mocking her.

"I'm not even going to try to get to know you. I refuse to name you and I'm *not* going to fall in love. Not this time!"

"Who're you talking to, baby?" Annika mumbled from under the covers.

Deciding to ignore the cat in favor of a warm and sleepy Annika, Jo dived back under the covers and proceeded to thoroughly kiss and love her mate awake.

When Jo emerged from beneath the covers a second time that morning, she found the cat had moved from the end of the bed to the armchair in the corner, where it perched and watched her silently.

"Seriously?" Jo demanded. "You're cute and all, but I've given up on familiars, so you can move on to the next person."

Annika threw the covers back and peeked up at Jo. "There's another cat already?"

Jo nodded toward the armchair and Annika let out a squeal of delight when she saw the black beauty waiting there. "She's gorgeous! Come on, Jo, let's make friends."

Jo sighed. "Fine."

The minute she approached, the cat leapt into her arms, purring loudly.

"She's so sweet." Annika burrowed into Jo's side, leaned over and kissed the cat on the head, then straightened and kissed Jo too.

Endless moments later, they both came up for air, gasping for breath, woozy from the heated spell they'd managed to cast together.

"You're dangerous," Annika gasped.

Jo giggled. "No more dangerous than you." She leaned in and kissed Annika one more time, then pulling back just a little, murmured against her lips, "Let's go find out if this kitten is meant for us or if she's just making a pit stop on her way elsewhere."

It didn't take long for the answer to arrive in the form of Jared and Corwin, the alpha and beta wolf shifters Pippa and Natalie had mated.

It was just luck—good or bad, Jo wasn't certain—that Natalie and Corwin arrived downstairs at the same time Pippa and Jared walked through the front door.

Styx—because Annika couldn't bear to leave the cat unnamed—immediately freaked out.

She leapt into the air, let out a series of hisses and growls, then skittered under the couch, where she crouched and growled at anyone who came near.

It took Jo an hour to coax her out from under the couch and she only managed it because Jared and Corwin finally left Coven House entirely.

"I suppose you could try and get her used to the wolves," Natalie said as Jo cuddled Styx in her arms, soothing her gently. "Maybe introduce them slowly over time."

"She's already been traumatized," Jo said. "Corwin lives here now and Jared and the pack visit often. I'm not putting her through that. It would be cruel. The only problem is I don't know who to ask this time. I can't give her to the wolves and we've already sent one cat to the chameleons and another to the vampires."

"How about Mr. Higgins in town?" Pippa suggested.

"Who?"

"He owns the hardware store. I heard his cat passed away a couple months ago. Maybe he's ready for another one."

As it turned out, Mr. Higgins was thrilled. "I've been thinking of getting another cat. Actually, I was thinking I might get two, so they wouldn't be lonely when I'm at work. You wouldn't happen to have another cat, would you?"

"Not yet," Jo said, "but maybe in a couple days."

"Well, definitely keep me in mind if you do."

After bidding their goodbyes to Styx and leaving the hardware store, Pippa scolded Jo. "You can't go putting that out there."

"Putting what out there?"

"This idea that you might have another cat available in a couple days. It implies you think the next cat won't be the right one for you either. You have to think positive. It'll happen, Jo. You just have to give it time."

"You sound like Annika," Jo said.

Pippa smiled. "Your Annika's the best thing that ever happened to you."

"She really is," Jo agreed.

"She makes sense, so you should listen to her."

"I'll try. It's just hard, you know? It's beginning to feel like I'm not meant to have a familiar."

"I'm sure that's not true, Jo. Just think of it as if you're a gateway for all these other cats to find their forever homes. Once they're taken care of, it'll be your turn. I'm sure of it."

It was time for Soraya to implement the next step in her marvelously *brilliant* plan. Step one was already complete and it had been a rousing success.

Unfortunately, step two required getting the other cats on board.

She was pretty sure they wouldn't approve, but she wasn't going to let that stop her.

Not liking Merry was no reason to deny her the efforts of the matchmaking cats of the goddesses. Merry deserved her happily ever after just as much as anyone else.

Besides, Merry was one of the most interesting people (demons), Soraya had ever known.

So as far as she was concerned, the other cats were just being unreasonable.

Like in the diner the other day when Merry was whispering with Starlight's daughter. The cats were convinced Merry was up to no good, corrupting the child or something, but Soraya was certain whatever they'd been discussing was purrfectly innocent.

She'd attempted to eavesdrop, but Merry was tricky and there was no listening in, even for a matchmaking cat of the goddesses.

Even worse was when they caught Merry conversing with Kyrie.

"Why is she talking to Satan's kitty?" Bygul had

demanded. "She's conspiring with her, I know she is. Oh, my goddess, this is bad."

Such a drama king.

Soraya was certain that conversation was purrfectly innocent as well.

It was that kind of prejudice though, that made Soraya determined to turn their efforts to matching Merry next.

After all, if the matchmaking cats of the goddesses weren't willing to try their paws at matching the half-devil, quarter-witch, quarter-fairy daughter of Satan, who in all the realms would?

With this in mind, Soraya prepared to implement her most genius plan ever, involving the waiting room and a whole lot of kittens.

All she had to do now was wait for the purrfect opening and when Muezza declared their latest match-making attempt, "purrfectly depressing," she knew her moment had arrived.

Twitching her tail in anticipation, digging deep for the drama she was so well known for, Soraya opened her mouth and let out a wail worthy of Queen Nefertiti herself. "This is a disaster! Who knew one witch could be so difficult?"

"Let's be clear," Muezza said. "It's not the witch."

"It's the wolves," Tivali said sourly. "Not to mention the demoness."

"It's all of them, including Jo," Bygul said impatiently. "She should have accepted the original familiar we chose for her."

"The plant-eater?" Tivali exclaimed incredulously.

"Buttercup," Soraya said. "His name's Buttercup."

"Yes, the plant-eater," Bygul said, then added impatiently when it looked like Soraya might interrupt again, "*Buttercup.*"

"He destroyed her garden," Tivali exclaimed.

"Well, maybe she's entirely too attached to her garden," Bygul said, "especially since the coven already has a houseful of cats constantly uprooting them."

"Yes, but those cats aren't bonded with Jo. She needs her own familiar, and one that isn't constantly destroying everything her magic creates," Tivali said.

"I think we should take a break," Soraya said. "Focus on a different witch for a while."

"Really?" Muezza said. "We've only tried three cats. Surely, we can take the time to try a few more."

"Yes, but hear me out. We're trying so hard with Jo, but we keep choosing wrong. Maybe we're too close to the situation and need to take a step back, focus on a different witch, just for a little while."

"She does have a point," Muezza said.

"Maybe a bit of time away would give us the clarity we need," Tivali agreed.

"Fine," Bygul sighed. "In that case—"

Before he could suggest a different witch, Soraya blurted out, "So, I know you guys are totally against this, but I really think our next match should be Merry."

"*Merry?*" Bygul, Muezza and Tivali all exclaimed at once.

"Not this *again*," Bygul groaned.

"She's a psycho," Muezza said.

"She is not!" Soraya said hotly. "She's funny and I like her and she deserves a happily ever after."

"She's not really a member of the coven," Bygul protested, "which means she's not even on our list. I thought we were going to focus on the necromancer next."

"Are you crazy?" Tivali exclaimed.

It took entirely too long to convince the other cats that Merry should be their next target witch, but once they agreed, Soraya's plan moved forward at light speed.

First, she transported the box of kittens.

It wasn't hard to find the box.

There were always abandoned kittens to be found somewhere.

In this case, this particular box was left in the middle of a rest stop about a hundred miles to the north of Merry's current location.

It wasn't difficult at all moving the box so that Merry found it, quick and easy.

Tivali scolded Soraya for not following procedures, but Soraya didn't care. After all, she had a plan and it was a truly brilliant one.

What followed was a whole lot of chaos and fun in Jamesville with Merry, a bunch of shifters and witches, and a crazy amount of black cats and kittens.

Soraya considered the entire experience a monumental success, one they'd desperately needed to regain their confidence after all those failures with Jo.

And so it was with a renewed sense of purpose that Soraya and the other matchmaking cats of the goddesses returned to the waiting room, to select another candidate for their target witch.

Four

T HE WAITING ROOM

"The portal was a truly brilliant idea, Soraya," Tivali said as they both stared at the box that sat in the middle of the waiting room, a box that for a short period of time had become a portal between the waiting room and a Shenanigans bar in Jamesville.

"Thanks, Tivali. I just can't believe Grumpy Cat never went into the box, not even once."

"You do realize he's dark gray, not black, right?" Muezza asked.

"Well, sure, but he's a cat. He should have at least investigated the box. Besides, I didn't *only* set the portal for black cats and kittens on our caseload. I *also* set it for Grumpy Cat specifically. He's so stubborn, though. I think he must have known what I was up to."

"And what exactly *were* you up to, Soraya?" Tivali asked.

"I was trying to find his furever home, of course."

"Well, it didn't work," Bygul said. "Are we choosing a different cat or are you going to try your luck with Grumpy Cat again, first?"

"Try my luck, of course." Soraya sauntered across the room, getting within two feet of Grumpy Cat before quickly backtracking when he lashed out, claws extended.

"Okay, okay, sorry, sorry. Maybe next time." Soraya hurried back to Bygul and the others, where she found them waiting with a black and white cat.

She scowled at them. "You didn't even wait to see if I'd have any luck, did you?"

"Of course not," Muezza said. "It's obvious that particular cat isn't going anywhere. I'm rather convinced he likes it here in the waiting room."

Soraya thought about that a moment, struck by the idea that a cat might actually want to *stay* in the waiting room, but then dismissed the thought as absurd.

Three days had passed since Jo gave Styx to Mr. Higgins.

Three days of no cats appearing in the Coven House, which left her feeling bereft, as if she'd been abandoned by the goddesses.

Annika tried to assure her that it was probably only temporary, but none of them really knew whether that was true or not. They didn't even know whether the goddesses were involved in the arrival of the three cats in the first place.

Jo had almost convinced herself that it was all just a coincidence when she woke on the third morning after giving away Styx, to find a cat staring down at her from the top of her canopy bed.

He was sitting on one of the four posts, as still and regal as a statue.

"How in the world did you get up there?" Jo demanded.

Of course, the cat didn't answer, but the moment Jo sat up and lifted her arms, he dove down into them.

He was a hefty armful, so Jo was glad she'd been sitting down when he landed in her arms and sent her toppling backward.

She landed next to Annika in an explosion of giggles.

Annika woke and immediately started fawning all over the cat. "You are so cute," she crooned to the cat. "What are we going to name you? Let's see."

"No, Annika." Jo closed her eyes. "We shouldn't name him. I'm probably going to have to give him to Mr. Higgins and it will just be better if I don't get attached."

"I know Mr. Higgins wants another cat, but there are cats everywhere. Why can't you keep this one? Who cares if it turns out he's not the perfect familiar? He can still be your companion. Right?"

Jo hesitated, then nodded. "Right. Humans have pet companions all the time. Why can't I?"

"Exactly! That's the spirit." Annika leaned over and kissed Jo, sending heat sweeping through them both and erasing any thoughts of cats for quite some time.

"So. Names," Annika gasped a lifetime later as they lay cuddling in the aftermath of their loving. "What things are black and white?" She reached out and stroked the cat, who had finally returned to the bed after deciding it was safe once more.

He sniffed Annika's fingers, then sniffed Jo's before stretching out beside them.

"Well, we can't name him cow because that would be ridiculous," Jo said.

"Let's see… zebras, dice, dominoes, Oreos."

"Oreos!" they said together.

"That's perfect," Jo said to Oreo, "because you're the sweetest thing ever."

Unfortunately, when they finally climbed out of bed, they discovered his sweetness only lasted as long as Jo didn't use her magic.

Any magic at all.

The tiniest of spells, one that made the bed, set him off in a massive way.

Oreo went nuts, attacking the bed and the pillows, shaking them and dragging them off the bed one-by-one.

"That's not a good sign," Annika observed.

"Not at all," Jo agreed. "If it's the magic setting him off, there's no way we can keep him. He'd go insane living with a bunch of witches."

By the time they finished getting ready for the day, they both knew this cat was no witch's familiar. Even worse, he wasn't a witch's companion cat either.

"It's not that bad," Jo said at breakfast to the rest of the Coven. She'd had enough time to process and she'd decided that Oreo would be much happier with Mr. Higgins. "At least, Styx will have a playmate now."

"Are you sure he senses magic?" Natalie asked. "Maybe it's something else he's sensing, something we can get rid of."

"Doubtful," Jo said, "especially considering how things went down with all the other cats."

"She's right," Annika said. "It's not like Jo could just get rid of all her plants and gardens."

"Or that I'd ever send Kyrie back to hell," Tempest said.

"More's the pity," Matthew muttered.

"Hey!" Tempest exclaimed. "Kyrie's a sweetheart."

"Right." Matthew glanced around the room warily. "And just where is this sweetheart again?"

Tempest shrugged. "She's around here somewhere."

Matthew let out a yelp and jerked back from the table. "She bit me!" he accused Tempest.

Tempest raised an eyebrow, looked under the table and crooned, "Aw. There you are, Kyrie. Come on up here, baby."

The hell-cat leapt onto Tempest's lap and from there onto the new dining room table, where she strutted from one end to the other, nodding regally to each person seated there.

"Freaky," Corwin muttered.

Tempest glared at him.

"Careful, Corwin, or I'll let Jo banish wolves from Coven House, just to keep the kitties happy," Natalie said.

"Anyway," Jo said as Kyrie strutted past her and Annika, both of them braving hell-kitty teeth to smooth a hand down Kyrie's sleek back as she stalked by. "The point is we couldn't get rid of my plants, or Kyrie, or the wolves, and now, we can't get rid of magic, so after dinner, we'll take Oreo here to Mr. Higgins and that'll be the end of that."

"I think we should test things out before giving up," Pippa said. "We can conduct a couple experiments, cast a few spells, see if maybe Oreo will acclimate to the magic."

"That's a wonderful idea," Natalie said.

It *wasn't* a wonderful idea.

A single spell after breakfast to clear the table convinced *everyone* that Oreo was not the cat for Jo.

Fur standing on end, leaping and twisting in mid-air, hissing and spitting at nothing, poor Oreo was a whirlwind of motion and *emotion*.

"He really does sense the magic," Natalie marveled.

"I told you," Jo said, "and I've decided I'm done with this game. Every time I think I've found the perfect familiar for me, I end up having to give him or her away. I'm never trying again. The next cat that shows up is for someone else, not for me."

Annika pulled Jo into her arms and hugged her tight. "I'm so sorry, my love," she whispered in Jo's ear. "We'll let someone else attempt the bonding next time."

"At least Mr. Higgins will be happy."

"I've been thinking," Soraya announced.

"Not again, Soraya!" Tivali exclaimed.

"I think we should match Jasmine with a kitten or two. She'd be thrilled, I'm sure."

"Who's Jasmine?" Bygul asked.

"Starlight's daughter."

"You *know* we don't involve children in our match-making efforts, Soraya," Bygul said sternly. "We can't be breaking children's hearts when their parents refuse to allow them to keep the cats."

"I know, but I'm sure Starlight wouldn't do that."

"There's no guarantee of that and you know it," Tivali said.

"Besides, I doubt we'll have to match Jasmine at all," Muezza said.

"Why's that?" Soraya asked.

"She's been working on a letter to Santa."

"Ohh." The other cats exclaimed.

"That's purrfect," Tivali said.

"As long as Santa Kitty doesn't get involved," Bygul said sourly.

"But I also wanted to match her mom," Soraya wailed.

"What?" Bygul, Tivali and Muezza exclaimed.

"She deserves a happily ever after too," Soraya said.

"We can't possibly match every single citizen of Zero, Kansas, Soraya," Bygul said. "We committed to the witches and that's all. We need to get serious about finding the right familiar for Jo or we're never going to finish with this Coven."

"Fine," Soraya said.

"I think we should stop letting the humans see the cats, at least until we know for sure they're not going to freak out. The cats, that is," Muezza said.

"That's a great idea," Tivali said. "I feel so bad for Jo every time it doesn't work out."

"We've never had such difficulty matching a cat before," Soraya said. "Do you think our goddess magic is failing us?"

The four cats looked at each other in silence for a moment, then as one, they all said, "Nah."

For the next several weeks, they tried cat after cat, with no success whatsoever.

The only part that *was* successful was their ability to mask the cats' presence in the coven house so that Jo was spared the additional heartbreak of bonding with yet more cats, only to discover they weren't the right fit for her.

Most of the cats they brought in attacked Jo's plants as if it was their mission in life to destroy her gardens.

It required quite a bit of goddess magic to heal the plants fast enough that Jo never noticed what was happening.

The few cats who *didn't* attack her plants were busy growling at the witches or the wolves or the magic the witches wielded, or on one memorable occasion, the other cats.

All of them.

That particular situation made absolutely no sense to Bygul since the cat in question had come from the waiting room, where he had co-existed with hundreds of other cats without a single issue.

The minute they transported him to the witches' coven house, though, he threw himself into defending that territory against any and all intruders, including the other cats who'd already laid claim to the territory.

Since the other cats couldn't see him stalking them, chaos had been the result.

Even worse was that he also perceived Bygul and the others as intruders and had viciously attacked them whenever they came near, thus delaying his return as they attempted to coordinate their efforts to catch him again.

After much trial and error, they finally managed to pin him to the floor and transport him back to the waiting room.

"I can't *believe* you," Tivali said in disgust when upon arrival, the cat simply settled on his side and began calmly grooming himself, not at all perturbed at the other cats, *hundreds* of them, milling about.

"Make a note," Bygul said wearily. "This one goes to a one-cat home."

SEVERAL WEEKS HAD PASSED SINCE OREO HAD shown up and Jo had given him to Mr. Higgins as a companion to Styx.

No other cats had arrived in that time.

This left Jo feeling both sad and grateful.

It felt as if the universe had heard her announcement that the next cat would be for someone else and had just gotten on with that, leaving Jo without any hope for her own familiar.

Jo had tried to spend her Thanksgiving holiday being thankful for all the blessings in her life, but most especially for Annika, her beautiful, wonderful, compassionate, *sexy* mate.

Jo had tried *not* to think about her hopes for a familiar and how they'd been dashed over and over again.

However, when she and Annika stopped at the diner one Saturday afternoon for a late lunch, and Starlight's daughter, Jasmine, whispered to Jo that she was writing a letter to Santa to ask for a kitten for Christmas, Jo wished desperately for a bit of that shining faith she saw in little Jasmine's eyes. That deep-rooted belief that if she only asked, she would surely gain her heart's desire.

That night, Jo made a wish for the same. She'd whispered to the night sky her wish for the perfect familiar.

She then joined Annika in bed, where they spent the night, indulging their passions together.

The heat and true bliss of making love with her mate shoved all thoughts of a familiar from Jo's head as she reveled in the joy of their mate bond.

"We've got a situation." Tivali arrived in a rush, a frantic look on her face. "Jasmine's letter has disappeared."

"But that's supposed to happen, right?" Soraya asked. "Letters addressed to Santa go to him."

"Not if they're not posted, they don't," Tivali said, "and apparently, Jasmine's mother never mailed it because she was planning to open it and read it herself."

"A lot of parents do that," Bygul said. "I'm not sure why it's a crisis."

"Because she can't find it and I'm guessing that means it's in Santa Kitty's hands right now."

All four cats groaned.

"I'll take care of this," Soraya said decisively, then popped away before Bygul could stop her.

"Great," he muttered.

"You know," Muezza said, "there's another option besides Santa Kitty. Personally, I'm betting on one of Satan's daughters, probably the fairy."

"*Merry?*" Bygul and Tivali exclaimed.

"We did see her hanging out with Starlight and Jasmine right before she left town," Muezza said.

"What would Merry want with a letter to Santa?" Tivali demanded.

"To cause chaos?" Muezza suggested. "She's a demon-witch-fairy hybrid, for goddess' sake. If anyone specializes in chaos, it would be her."

At that moment, Soraya popped back in. "I have good news and bad news." She then proceeded to tell them that Santa Kitty did *not* have the letter after all.

Satan did.

Five

T HE HOLIDAYS ARRIVED quickly, as they always did, which meant that life became a bit hectic for Jo and the rest of the coven as they frantically attempted to do all the things.

Christmas lights for those of them who celebrated Christmas.

The menorah in the window and the lighting of the candles for Amaryllis and Rowan.

And some Yuletide blessings for the rest of them.

It was an eclectic holiday season with a lot of laughter and fabulous parties.

They also had some fun new experiences, on account of the mates.

No, not Annika.

The *other* mates.

The Christmas lights were a prime example.

Jo and the other witches used their magic to hang the lights the year before, and Jo could honestly say, she'd never seen a more beautiful sight in her life once they were finished.

This year, though, hanging the lights by magic apparently was not acceptable. At least, not according to the wolves, who insisted they be hung the old-fashioned way.

Worse, they refused to allow the women to hire anyone to accomplish that task, and instead insisted they'd handle it themselves.

Apparently it was a rite of passage involving too much testosterone and male foolishness.

Much to Tempest's disgust, the wolves managed to rope Matthew into helping them with their lighting mission.

This led to the women standing around, wincing and yelling and occasionally offering (i.e., begging) to, "Cast just one tiny, little spell. We promise it'll help."

"No!" was the answer every single time.

When it became clear that watching three grown-ass men crawl around on a roof while attempting to untangle Christmas lights because they were too stupid to do that while on the ground, was just an exercise in terror and frustration, the women retired inside to drink lots and lots of wine.

Eventually, the lights were hung and if they weren't exactly straight and if one strand didn't work at all, well, it was the thought that counted.

They celebrated a pseudo-successful lighting ceremony with more wine and lots of food.

Jo and Annika stumbled to bed in the wee hours of the morning, giggling over the ridiculousness of men and congratulating themselves for *never, ever* having to deal with that kind of testosterone bullshit in their own relationship.

It was a wonderful revelation and one they promised each other they'd never forget.

"Let's be grateful forever," Jo said drunkenly.

"Forever," Annika agreed.

The rest of the holiday season flew by and before they knew it, they were celebrating New Year's Eve in the wolf den, a celebration unlike any other.

"I had no idea wolves were so damn goofy," Annika observed.

"So goofy," Jo agreed.

As the night wore on and the drinking accelerated, clothes became optional as wolves decided to shift back and forth from human to wolf to human again.

When human, they tended to howl for no reason

whatsoever and when wolfy, they seemed to enjoy chasing their own tails entirely too much.

Then someone brought out a karaoke machine and things just went downhill from there.

Jared and Corwin led the way to a small stage in the back yard, where they stood with five other wolves, three of them in wolf form, surrounded by snow, and prepared to sing their hearts out.

"How are the wolves going to sing?" Annika muttered in Jo's ear.

Jo shook her head. "I still can't get over the fact that these wolves love karaoke. Look at them. They're practically vibrating with excitement."

"Maybe they're all excellent singers," Morana suggested. "It's possible we're about to be blown away by the musical talents of the pack."

"I'll believe it when I hear it," Natalie muttered.

That's when the wolves began to sing.

Or howl.

Whatever it was they were doing, it *wasn't* excellent.

The song mainly consisted of howling.

The freakiest part was that the wolves in human form sounded as wild as those in wolf form. The howls actually gave Jo chills.

The rest of the performance though?

Sad.

"Awooooooo, full moon's a-coming! Awooooooo, embrace the wildness! Awoooooooo!" Every time they howled, the human wolves tossed back their heads and looked about as feral as a human might ever look.

"Awooooooo, wild wolves a-coming! Awooooooo, let me hear you howl!"

Jo and Annika both jumped when all the wolves in the audience howled with the wolves on stage. "Awoooooooo! Awoooooooo!"

"Good goddess," Pippa muttered.

Jo clenched her jaw tight and stared straight ahead, afraid if she caught the eyes of even one coven member, she would lose it.

Annika squeezed her hand tighter and tighter.

Jo peeked out of the corner of her eye and saw that Annika looked about ready to explode.

"Gotta go!" Jo took off through the crowd, dragging Annika behind her. They hit the back door, raced through the den house and out the front.

They ran down the front drive all the way to the end of the block where their car was parked.

Jo beeped the locks early, so that when they reached the car, she jerked open the back door, nudged Annika inside, dove in after her and slammed the door shut.

The minute they were enclosed in the car, Jo and Annika exploded with laughter.

They fell into each other, laughing hysterically.

Just when they'd start to sober up, one of them would burst into laughter again and they'd be off.

"Did-did you see the way they threw their heads forward and then back every time they howled to the moon?" Annika giggled.

"Or when Jared started jumping around the stage, waving his arms at the audience, getting them all riled up, just so they could howl some more?"

They both burst into laughter again.

"I had no idea men could be so entertaining," Annika said. "Do you think they're all like that or is it just the wolves?"

"Not a clue, but I have to say I'm *so* grateful I'm not Natalie or Pippa tonight."

"Well, I mean, obviously because they're mated to guys, ew, but why else?"

"Because they're not just mated to any guys. They're mated to *those* guys, the ones who were howling like rock stars on a stage."

"Yeah, so?"

"So, Natalie and Pippa are going to have to pretend they *liked* that song. They're going to have to *compliment* them."

They both burst into laughter again.

"Natalie?" Annika exclaimed. "Do you *really* think Natalie's going to compliment Corwin's singing?"

"Okay, probably not Natalie, but Pippa? Yeah, she's going to pretend she loved that song."

"You know what else?"

"What?"

"When Jared comes at her, all revved up from the performance and howling at the moon, she'll welcome him with open arms and if he's any good, she may just *encourage* him to sing next time around."

"Oh, dear goddess." Jo stared at Annika and they both giggled some more.

"I'm so damn glad I'm not straight," Annika said.

"Hallelujah to that," Jo said, then kissed Annika breathless.

They lay in the backseat, talking and cuddling, kissing and stroking each other until the sounds of voices had them straightening their clothes, kissing one last time, then climbing into the front seat for the drive home.

It was only a ten minute drive, but they held hands the entire way.

After spending Christmas *and* New Year's in the Hell Realm, managing a truly challenging match involving vampires, humans, witches, the devil himself and a whole lot of hell-kittens, Bygul was ready to give up and go home to the goddesses.

No more mate-matching, cat-matching or any kind of matching for him.

At least not for another seventy-two years.

That was the plan, but then he remembered Jo back in Zero, Kansas, and the quest for the purrfect familiar.

Bygul wasn't a cat to leave a job unfinished, no matter how difficult, or interminable, it happened to be. He glared at Soraya, the one cat he blamed for all the delays in this particular case.

"What?" Soraya exclaimed when she noticed him glaring. "What did I do?"

"I don't know how you're managing it, but you need to stop manipulating us," Bygul said.

"I would never!"

"Really? Because somehow, we always seem to end up matching people not on our list, Soraya," Bygul said severely. "People *you* keep suggesting. *Then*, even though we all agree that we can't possibly take on anyone else right now, the situation somehow gets twisted in such a way that our expertise is required, and the next thing we know, we're matching your suggestions anyway. Well, no more! We have a list and we're sticking to it this time, starting with Jo!"

"I don't know what you're going on about, Bygul," Soraya said innocently. "I may have suggested a few people, it's true, but I haven't done anything to push them to the top of the list. I've always been willing to wait until after we finish matching the coven. If others suddenly take priority, that has nothing to do with me. It must be goddess magic at work."

Bygul eyed her suspiciously.

Goddess magic.

Right.

Goddess magic wielded by Soraya, no doubt.

"Fine. Let's just focus on finding a familiar for Jo, shall we?" He said this even as he was aware he'd said it many times before, yet somehow, they'd ended up in Jamesville, matching that crazy demon-witch-fairy, and then in *Hell,* matching a human with a vampire.

What next?

Lucifer himself?

They spent the rest of January testings cats with Jo, but for some reason, no matter what cat they tried, it was never a purrfect match.

January was coming to a close and Bygul was

running out of patience when they reconvened in the waiting room for one more attempt.

"Who should we choose this time?" He asked wearily as felines raced around the cavernous room, playing and wrestling and chasing each other up and down cat trees and through tunnels.

"At this point, I don't have a clue," Tivali said.

"We've never had this much difficulty matching a human with a cat before," Muezza agreed.

"I'm beginning to think Jo may be right," Soraya said morosely. "Maybe there isn't a familiar for her."

Even though Bygul was starting to think the same thing—maybe they'd finally met an unmatchable—he would never admit it to his team. Shoving aside his weariness, he drew in a deep breath and gave them the company line.

"Absolutely *no one* is unmatchable, not a cat and not a human," Bygul said. "The trouble is that we've gotten lazy because all our matches have been relatively easy. We need to remember that witches are the hardest matches we'll ever make. It's not enough for them to fall in love with a cat. The cat has to be able to tap into the witch's magic. The two have to bond so that the witch's magic grows in power.

"While any cat can be a companion, not every companion can be a witch's familiar. It's our job to see the cats for who they truly are and find the purrfect companion for each of them. If a cat isn't meant to be a familiar, they're not the right companion for a witch."

"That's why it doesn't make any sense," Soraya wailed.

"What doesn't?" Bygul asked.

"Grumpy Cat."

Tivali groaned. "Seriously? This cat again?"

"I'm telling you, he's a familiar. I can sense the magic all over him. He's definitely meant for greater things. I really think he's supposed to be with Jo."

"Well, let's try to convince him again, then," Bygul said.

Muezza and Tivali let out twin sounds of annoyance, but they followed Soraya and Bygul across the room to where Grumpy Cat was sprawled on a ledge, glaring out at the world.

"You try this time, Bygul," Soraya said. "Maybe he just doesn't like me, though I really can't imagine why."

Bygul wasn't sure he wanted to try to convince this stubborn cat of anything, mostly because he didn't enjoy failing and he was sure from the way the dark gray cat was eyeing him, failure was guaranteed.

Five minutes later, ears laid back, tail twitching

furiously and missing about ten thousand strands of fur, Bygul stalked away from an angry, hissing Grumpy Cat and snapped, "That one," to the other cats as he stormed by.

"Which one did he mean?" Soraya asked.

"His tail twitched that way," Muezza said.

They all turned and stared at a small, gray-striped tabby who had watched the cat fight while hunched close to the ground and now stared at them warily.

"Well, come along then," Soraya said, brushing up against the tabby and nudging her forward. "Time to find your furever home."

THE LAST DAY OF JANUARY DAWNED WITH snow blanketing every surface outside and a charming, winter hush enclosing the world.

Of course, the coven immediately changed all their plans in favor of playing outside in the snow.

Jo helped Annika slather her skin in the strongest sun screen on the market and bundle up so very little skin was showing. "Are you sure you want to go outside?" Jo asked worriedly. "The sun is always brighter when there's snow on the ground and even with the scarf and the face mask, I can still see a bit of skin."

"It'll be fine, Jo. The worst that can happen is I'll be beat red for a day or two. Totally worth it to play in the sun with my mate."

They grinned at each other, then clasping hands, raced down the stairs and out the front door to join the coven in an epic snowball battle.

They ran and played in the snow, the witches using spells to throw snowballs at ridiculous speeds, thus giving them a terribly unfair advantage they thoroughly enjoyed by pummeling the men into submission.

When they were all exhausted and had collapsed in the snow to make snow angels, Pippa stood above them and announced, "We should build a snow village."

"Oooh, what kind of village?" Natalie asked.

"I'm thinking a replica of Zero downtown."

This, right here, with her coven, was what made Jo so grateful to be a witch.

With her powers, she was able to call forth the tiniest of sprouts buried in the snow, to make it grow into miniature replicas of the trees in the town square.

Tempest stirred the wind to roll giant balls of snow into the center of their village that everyone worked on hollowing out and squaring off, forming the buildings of Zero, Kansas.

They stacked and packed snow, forming roads and streetlights and buildings and people.

Once they finished building the town square, Jo and Annika focused on recreating Library Zero, while a few doors down, Corwin and Natalie worked on Zero Diner.

"Starlight's almost finished," Natalie announced.

"So's Jasmine," Morana said from the street corner, where she'd been working on a replica of a school bus. She was now shaping the little girl's hair. Jasmine appeared to be mid-stride as she crossed the street toward the diner where her mother worked.

Curiosity led Jo to peek inside the diner, where she could see Starlight standing between tables, plates of food in each hand.

"Wow," Annika said, as they watched Natalie carefully shape a tiny sausage link and float it into the diner to settle on top of one of the plates. "Does she realize it's all going to melt eventually?"

Jo snickered. "It's not about when it melts, it's about the joy of building it in the first place."

Glancing around at the rest of their village, Jo realized while she'd been carefully making miniature stacks of books to place on the shelves inside the library, the others had begun working on some of the other inhab-itants of Zero, Kansas.

She recognized Mr. Higgins standing outside his hardware store and—oh, my goddess. Pippa had added Styx and Oreo playing at his feet. So cute!

"We need a few accessories for our snow people," Annika said. "I'll go grab a few." She went to turn away, but Jo grabbed her hand and pulled her back. "How are you feeling?" Annika had ditched the face mask, scarf and coat a while back, as had most of them, and was now looking a bit red in the face. It was hard to tell whether that was from the sun or the wind though.

Annika beamed at Jo. "I'm fine. I'm going to get our phones too. We need pictures of this magic." She leaned in and kissed Jo sweetly.

Jo immediately wrapped her arms around Annika and pulled her closer, the world fading around them as they lost themselves in the magic of each other.

"WHAT IN THE WORLD?" SORAYA BREATHED IN amazement, trying to take in everything around them all at once.

Jo was standing in the middle of what looked to be

miniature buildings made entirely of snow. She was using a stick to write words on the front of one.

"Library Zero," Tivali read. "It's the village. They've built the entire downtown area of Zero out of snow!"

"But *why?*" Bygul exclaimed.

"Who cares?" Muezza exclaimed. "Look at this building. It's cat-sized." He ran inside Zero Grocery and back out again, darting across the miniature street into Zero Hardware next.

Kyrie, Cookie, Hocus Purrcus and Moonbeam were all racing through the village, kicking up snow and playing like kittens. Despite racing in and out of buildings, much the way Muezza was, they managed not to knock a single building over.

"Come on, guys," Muezza called. "How often do you get to have your own cat-sized village to play in?"

Soraya let out a happy meow and raced after him, Tivali and the little tabby they'd transported with them following along.

"Oh, come on," Bygul called after them. "We're here to work, not play."

"Join us, Bygul," Soraya yelled. "The snow feels fantastic!"

Bygul hesitated for a long moment before saying, "Fine, but ten minutes *only*." With that, he bounded forward and for the next ten minutes, he romped and played with the other cats and allowed all his worries to fall away.

He felt so much more relaxed when the ten minutes were up and he and the other matchmaking cats gathered in the miniature town square to observe the little tabby.

She raced through the snow with the other cats, weaving in and out of the humans still working on the village while sniffing everything.

"This cat's promising," Muezza said. "She hasn't freaked out yet. The entire coven's here *with* their mates."

"Yep," Soraya said. "She doesn't seem to mind the witches, wolves *or* chameleons."

"She also hasn't freaked out from the magic sending snow flying everywhere," Tivali said.

"We should let the humans see her now," Soraya said. "I bet Jo will absolutely adore her."

A few moments later, the tabby was winding her way through Jo's feet.

"Ohh, you're so beautiful. Where'd you come from, love?" Jo leaned down and picked up the tabby, cuddling her close.

"What'd I tell you?" Soraya asked. "They're a purr-fect match."

The front door of the coven house banged open and Jo's vampire mate, Annika, raced outside. "Sorry it took so long," she called and she ran across the lawn toward her mate. "It took me a while to track down the kitty lights." She held up a strand of lights in the shape of cats, then dropped them when she caught sight of the tabby in Jo's arms.

"Kitty!" Making a beeline for Jo, she reached out to pet the cat, who went from purring contentment to hissing and yowling and struggling to escape in an instant.

"Not again," Tivali groaned. "I can't believe we didn't notice Annika was missing."

"I can't believe the tabby's scared of Annika," Soraya wailed. "She's so sweet."

"She's also a vampire," Bygul pointed out. "The cat must have some highly developed survival instincts."

"*Please*. It's not like vampires *eat* cats or anything," Soraya said. She hesitated a moment. "They don't, right?"

"Of course not," Bygul exploded. "Satan would

destroy every last vampire in all the realms if they dared harm a single strand of fur on any cat's head."

"Oh, yeah, I forgot about him."

"How could you *possibly* forget about the second greatest cat protector in all the realms?" Muezza demanded. "After the goddesses, of course."

"I'm going to name her Fang," Jo announced to the coven as they walked inside, Jo doing her best to soothe Fang while Annika kept her distance. "Also, I'm going to give her to your mother." She nudged Jared's shoulder as she trooped past him and Pippa.

"*What?*" Bygul, Tivali Soraya, Muezza, Corwin and Jared all exclaimed together.

"*My* mother?" Jared asked.

"She's the perfect wolf candidate," Jo said. "You told us she loves Chester. I bet she'll be thrilled to have her very own cat to play with."

"Great," Corwin muttered. "More cats in the wolf den."

"Let's go introduce them right now," Pippa said. "Can we pretend it was my idea? I could really use some mother-in-law points."

"Of course, we can," Jo said. "I'm going to get cleaned up and then we'll head out. Meet back here in a few minutes?"

"You got it!" Pippa said cheerfully.

"I suppose we should go as well, just to make sure poor Fang adjusts to an entire den full of wolves," Bygul said. "We can also look in on Chester while we're there, not that he was on any matchmaker lists, but since he's living with wolves, it's probably a good idea to check on him now and again."

"Agreed," Tivali said.

A moment later, the four of them popped into the middle of the den's common area and found themselves surrounded by complete and utter chaos.

Jo, Pippa, Jared, Corwin and Natalie were all in Pippa's car, headed toward pack lands.

Annika had chosen to stay behind, simply because none of them wanted to traumatize Fang anymore than she already had been.

Fang and Hocus Purrcus were curled up together in the back window, Fang showing absolutely no evidence of her earlier trauma.

"Maybe I should have given her a bit more time to get used to Annika," Jo said. "We agreed we were going to keep the next cat, but how could we keep one who was terrified of her?"

"You're making the right decision," Natalie said.

"She's a beautiful kitty, but she's not the one for you. She'll be happy with the pack and your heart will be open when your true familiar finally arrives."

"Right," Jo muttered, wondering when all the platitudes would finally become reality.

"WHAT IS HAPPENING RIGHT NOW?" SORAYA exclaimed.

Wolves were chasing each other through the house, leaping through the air, snarling and barking at nothing. They raced out the front door, hurtled around the house, then barreled back inside to race up and down the stairs, through the hallways and back again, the sound of their paws a thunder that rumbled through the entire house.

Meanwhile, Chester stood on top of a cat tree, swatting at the wall.

There were a few wolves who *weren't* racing through the house. One of them was busy having a sneezing fit in the corner while another scratched furiously and whined.

At that moment, the witches arrived with Fang, Hocus Purrcus and the two wolves.

Jared and Corwin immediately transformed into

their wolf forms and joined the chase as it thundered outside once more.

As another wave of wolves hurtled toward them, Fang leapt from Jo's arms onto the back of one, then swatted something off its neck as they raced by.

Whatever it was flew through the air, slowed to a hover, then charged back again.

Pixies!" Soraya exclaimed.

"Where did they come from?" Bygul demanded. "There aren't any portals to Hell nearby."

"Ghosts! We've been invaded by ghosts!" A naked wolf shrieked as he raced by, waving his arms in the air.

Two pixies had his hair gripped in their fists, like they were holding the reins of a horse, squealing and laughing as his speed lifted them into the air so they were flying without using their wings.

"Pixies aren't ghosts." Soraya sounded disgusted.

"Yes, well, earthbound creatures can't exactly see them," Bygul said, "unless the pixie wants to be seen, of course."

"So, basically, the pixies are torturing the wolves," Muezza observed.

"Well, it is their specialty," Bygul said.

The wolf and Fang hurtled by again, the pixie Fang had dislodged now hanging from the wolf's tail.

From the look on Fang's face, it was clear he was having the time of his life.

"I'm pretty sure Fang's going to fit right in here with the wolves," Tivali observed.

Muezza let out a rumble of agreement.

"Do you think we should let them know the den's been infested with a bunch of pixies?" Soraya asked.

"Eh, there are only five of them," Muezza said. "Even if they have a couple babies, the wolves should be fine. A little freaked out, sure, but otherwise fine."

"Yeah, until their number reaches eight," Bygul said sourly.

"Not our problem," Tivali said decisively. "We have a crisis right now, one we've never experienced before. We're actually *failing* as matchmakers."

"I'm calling a team meeting," Bygul said abruptly.

A few moments later, they were all standing in a small office outside the waiting room.

"We need a new plan," Bygul said. "Something better than let's just try another cat. We could be trying cats from now to the end of days."

"Agreed," Tivali said, her tail twitching in annoyance, "This has been a disaster."

They debated and lamented and kept going back and forth about what to do until Soraya made the same suggestion she always did, that they turn their attention to someone else.

Bygul didn't even recognize the name of the woman she suggested. "Who?"

"The librarian," Muezza and Tivali said.

Bygul groaned. Didn't they already have this conversation?

Apparently they were going to have it again.

As they went back and forth, Soraya kept dropping little information bombs on them, like the fact that a couple of Satan's hell-kitties had escaped and were wandering Library Zero.

Soraya then informed them that she believed Jane, the *librarian*, for goddess' sake, was the purrfect match for Satan.

Bygul just shook his head as they popped over to the library. He fully intended to ignore Soraya's matchmaking plans in favor of capturing the hell-kitty fugitives and sending them back to Hell before Satan discovered them missing.

Unfortunately, it turned out that ship had already sailed. From there, things just went from bad to worse when Lucifer decided to kidnap the human librarian.

"For goddess' sake." Bygul scowled at Soraya. "This means we have to go back to Hell. *Again.*" How did she keep doing this? How was Soraya constantly ensuring that they ended up matching *exactly* who she wanted them to?

THE FIRST TWO weeks of February were uneventful for the coven.

Zero had a full week of sunny weather that ended up melting their snow village to nothing, though the cats had a couple days to play in the snow and to prance through the buildings before that happened.

Of course, the witches had taken pictures of the full village and each individual building with its carefully constructed snow people. They'd also taken pictures of the wolves and the cats running through the snow and posing inside the buildings, and of the cats posing on top of them, so it wasn't like the village was truly gone forever.

One of Jo's favorite pictures was of Fang standing

in front of the "window" of the hardware store, staring down at the snow cats, clearly contemplating whether he should attack them or not.

Another favorite photo was one Morana had captured of Jo and Annika kissing in the middle of the town square they'd built of snow.

The passion and love between them was obvious and made her heart clutch every time she looked at the photo.

She'd had it enlarged and framed and had it wrapped ready to present to Annika for Valentine's Day. She also made plans to take Annika out for dinner and to romance and woo her all day long.

Some might believe that once Jo and Annika had declared their love for one another, no romance *or* wooing was needed, but Jo maintained these were the necessary ingredients for happiness with her mate.

Romance and wooing were *always* required. With this in mind, she'd planned an entire day of fun activities perfect for wooing.

The morning of Valentine's Day, Jo woke to the sensation of an anvil sitting on her chest. When she opened her eyes, she found herself face-to-face with a huge, deeply dark, gray cat. His fur was so unrelentingly dark, it was just a shade away from black.

The cat was big, huge really, with a thick coat of

fur that wasn't exactly long, but wasn't short either. Thick, beautiful and so soft.

He was purring and the minute they made eye contact, he greeted her with a tiny lick of her nose.

"Oh, my goddess," she murmured. "You are the most beautiful cat I've ever seen in my life." Tears pricked her eyes at the thought of having to give this cat away too. Somehow, though, she knew deep inside, this one was meant for her.

Something inside her had unlocked the moment she caught sight of him. She could feel her magic bubbling up from her well, reaching for this cat, stroking tiny tendrils of magic along his spine, greeting him with joy.

Annika rolled over and opened her eyes at that moment. "Kitty," she whispered. With a shaking hand, she reached out and pet the cat's head.

The cat's purring got louder. He turned and licked Annika's fingers.

Annika giggled. "Oh, my goddess, Jo. He's perfect in every way!"

"Did you smuggle him in for Valentine's Day?" It suddenly occurred to Jo that Annika had known how much she wanted a cat and who better than her own mate to find the perfect familiar for her?

"No, I've never seen him before," Annika said.

"Besides, I wouldn't have a clue how to choose a cat for you. You always said your familiar would find you or you would find him. I think it's finally happened, Jo."

"I do too. I can feel it in my blood and my bones and my heart. He's lodged right here." She tapped her chest. "He's the key to unlocking the full power of my magic, but he's more than that. Annika, he's just perfect. I can't wait to introduce him to the rest of the Coven. They'll be so excited!"

The rest of the morning they spent with the Coven and the other cats, introducing Sir Alexander the Grey to everyone.

Jo had planned to take Annika out for Valentine's Day, but they decided instead to stay around Coven House, to give the cats a chance to play and get used to each other and to solidify Jo's growing bond with Alexander the Grey.

Therefore, instead of going out, they had a picnic lunch in the garden room at the back of the house, where Jo's plants blossomed and bloomed even in the middle of winter.

Alexander the Grey raced along the paths through the atrium, batting at vines with claws sheathed, rolling in the dirt and frolicking through the flowers. He placed his paws carefully everywhere he walked, as if he knew how important the gardens were to Jo, as if he could feel her magic in every grain of sand and dirt, in the tiniest of sprouts and the largest of leaves. He truly was the perfect cat familiar for her.

There, in the middle of Jo's inside gardens, surrounded by her magic in plant-form, with Alexander the Grey playing and dancing through the vines and flowers, Jo and Annika celebrated the beauty of their life together once more.

Vines grew and wrapped around them, cocooning them in their own world, cushioning their bodies as they rolled across the ground, stroking and kissing one another, the heat building around them, until there was nothing but each other and the endless tide that was their enduring love.

When Bygul and the other cats finally returned to the Earth realm and to the Zero Cum Laude Coven House, they found the entire coven hanging out in the living room.

Jo and Annika were cuddled together in a large armchair, both of them crooning at a cat in Jo's arms.

"Is that—is that," Bygul began.

"Grumpy Cat?" Soraya exclaimed.

"How is this possible?" Tivali demanded.

"How long were we in the Hell realm?" Bygul asked.

"Uh, does this box look familiar to anyone else?" Muezza asked. He was standing by the back door where a cardboard box stood, possibly waiting to be carted out of the house.

"That's the portal box," Soraya exclaimed, "the one from the Waiting Room. But I removed the black kitty spell a long time ago."

"What about the Grumpy Cat one?" Bygul asked.

"Oops."

"So why didn't the portal take him to Shenanigans in Jamesville?" Tivali asked.

"It's not like I cast a spell to just send cats into Jamesville willy-nilly," Soraya exclaimed. "There was a built-in failsafe."

"What kind of failsafe?" Bygul asked suspiciously.

"The kind that said if the kitty's purrfect match existed somewhere else in the earth realm, they'd be transported there instead."

"Soraya!" Tivali exclaimed. "What if that actually happened to some of our cats? We'd have had no way of tracking them."

"Silly. If any cats went anywhere but Jamesville, all we'd have to do is go through the portal ourselves. Goddess magic would have taken us right to them."

"Your portal is extremely complicated and I don't like it," Tivali said.

"Besides, if you can create a portal that sends cats to their purrfect companion, what are we good for?" Muezza asked. "You'll invent us right out of a job."

"Huh. Good point. I didn't think of that. Well, the good news is the magic's dormant now. All the target kitties have found their purrfect, furever homes, so it's just a box now."

"And you'll never make a portal like it again," Tivali said severely.

"Of course not," Soraya said. "It served its purpose. Building another one would just be boring."

"Well, I for one, cannot believe that Grumpy Cat was the purrfect familiar for Jo all along," Bygul said.

"I knew my instincts weren't that badly off," Soraya exclaimed. "What I can't understand is why he kept refusing to come with us in the first place. I swear, he was just being stubborn."

"He was being a *cat*," Bygul corrected. "Moving at his own pace, on *his* own timeline."

"Gotta respect that," Muezza said.

"Indeed," Bygul agreed.

ALEXANDER THE GREY WAS HAVING THE BEST day, not that he'd ever admit it, of course.

First, curiosity had finally gotten the better of him and, checking every which way to make sure no cats (*especially* not the goddess ones) were watching, he'd investigated the box.

The box where many cats and kittens had disappeared into, never to be seen again.

The box that chirpy, cheerful, *annoying* Siamese kept trying to get him to check out.

The box he was certain would mean his doom.

Even knowing this, though, eventually, inevitably, curiosity got the better of him.

Turned out, though, curiosity did *not*, in fact, kill the cat.

Instead, it led him to a house with other cats (boring—cats were the same everywhere) and *witches*.

Now witches were interesting.

Magic was interesting.

And magic that made plants grow was *amazing*.

Of course, Alexander the Grey didn't know about the plants until he was exploring the first floor and found the room at the back of the house filled with them.

It smelled amazing in there, so he'd spent quite a

bit of time exploring every inch of that room, sniffing every plant and climbing every tree.

Yes, there were trees *inside* the house!

Not cat trees.

No, these were real, live *trees*.

Magic.

After rubbing up against every plant and every tree in that room, Alexander the Grey was quite familiar with the feel of that magic, so of course, he had to follow its trail when it wandered away from the garden room.

That trail had led him up some stairs and down a hallway until he'd reached a door that was cracked open, just a little.

He'd slipped inside, following that magical trail to a bed, where he'd found two humans sleeping.

The minute Alexander the Grey had leapt onto the bed and seen the witch named Jo, sleeping there, he'd known she was his. His to train. His to care for. His to *rule*.

He'd immediately made himself comfortable on her chest and waited for her to wake.

When she had, she'd been thrilled to see him and he'd felt something inside, something dark and sad, brighten.

He'd then spent the best day with her and the vampire she called Annika.

Watching them together, he'd decided they were more one unit than two, which meant that Annika belonged to him too. She, too, was his to train and care for and rule.

Jannika, he decided. From now on, he'd call them Jannika.

Jannika introduced him to the other cats.

Again, *boring*.

Cats were all the same.

Even hell-cats.

The same.

They introduced him to two wolves and a chameleon, but again, *boring*.

Wolves: nothing but goofy dogs.

Definitely beneath his notice.

And the chameleon was just a fancy name for cat, so as far as Alexander the Grey was concerned, the chameleon was just like every other cat in the world.

By the end of the day, Alexander the Grey had divided all the inhabitants of the house into two categories: his and not his.

If they weren't his, he just didn't care.

Of course, the absolute best moment of the day was when that overly cheerful, chirpy, chatty Soraya showed up with her other cat friends and they all freaked out when they saw him draped across Jannika's laps, purring.

He didn't know *why* they were so surprised.

They were cats and everyone knows that cats can't be owned, so that meant every cat was in the category *not his.*

Of *course,* Alexander the Grey would purr for the ones who belonged to him.

Everyone else? Forget it.

Even if they *were* the matchmaking cats of the goddesses.

Wondering what the matchmaking cats of the goddesses were up to every time they abandoned their quest to find the purrfect familiar for Jo?

Check out their adventures on Pepper's website or read on for a sneak peek.

Now Leaving
ZERO, KANSAS
PLEASE
COME AGAIN!

CHOCOLATE

Excerpt

Furnanigans

This was so unfair.

Merry had spent years turning away the cutest kittens hell had ever spat out, then months in Zero, Kansas, pretending not to notice how adorable the coven's familiars were, resisting all temptation to try and score one for herself.

And look what she got for her efforts—an entire boxful of adorable kittens staring her in the face the moment she was on her own, with no one else to manipulate into taking responsibility for them.

Hands on hips, Merry glared down at the box and counted kittens.

She lost count several times due to the kittens' repeated attempts to climb the walls of the box only to tumble back down, usually knocking at least one other kitten down with them.

She thought there were six of them, but worst case scenario, there might actually be eight of the little buggers.

She groaned. "Fine. You can come with me, but don't get too comfortable." She scooped the box up and strode back to the car. "We'll be finding homes for each of you because I'm certainly not in the market for one kitten, let alone all y'all, no matter how adorable you may be."

She opened the passenger door and stood there staring.

Okay, now, this really *wasn't* fair.

The passenger seat was full of the best treats this gas station had to offer, leaving absolutely no room for a box of kittens. And the box was too tall to fit under the dash on the floorboard.

Seriously?

There was no help for it. She was going to have to move her stash because no way was Merry going to put the box of kittens in the backseat.

That would be a recipe for disaster.

She just knew the minute they were out of her sight, they'd somehow escape the box and then it would be invasion of the claws and the cat fur and the hairballs.

No, thank you.

Heaving a sigh of dejection, Merry shoved all the lovely treats onto the floor board and settled the box on the passenger seat. "Don't get used to it," she snarled.

"Mrawr," was the only response.

Grabbing two handfuls of treats, Merry closed the door and stalked around to the driver's side, examining what she held along the way.

Snickers—so good.

Reeses—always fabulous.

Raisinets—under normal circumstances, raisins were disgusting. However, in this case, Raisinets served as proof that chocolate made *everything* better.

Oreos—delicious bits of goodness that got stuck in her teeth, turning them black. Snacks for later!

She settled into the driver's seat, tossed most of the snacks onto the dash, retaining a box that apparently held Milk Duds inside.

She didn't understand the use of the word Dud in relation to chocolate, nor milk, to be honest.

After all, milk was rather disgusting. More proof that chocolate made everything better. Chocolate milk. Yum.

Five minutes down the road and Merry pulled onto the shoulder, executed a u-turn and returned to the gas station.

"Don't look at me like that," she said to the kittens as she climbed back into the car, dumping an armful of Milk Duds on top of the other treats on the floorboard. "If you'd tasted them, you'd have gone back too. Trust me, they're divine. But not good for kittens, which is good news for me, because that means, these are all mine. Paws off, kittens!"

Back on the road, she spent the next hour eating her way through pack after pack of Milk Duds—chewy, divine caramel covered in the greatest substance on earth, *chocolate*—and chatting with the kittens.

"Look, I know some humans are probably going to be terribly disappointed when they go into that gas station and realize that someone bought their entire stock of Milk Duds, but honestly, I deserve them more than any human on earth. After all, I have an entire lifetime of eating these treats to catch up on. How many years is that, anyway?" She thought about it a moment, trying to count, but decided she really just didn't care. "It's a lot of years, all right? And that means, a lot of Milk Duds still to consume before I've caught up to even one eight-year-old human!"

"Mrawr."

"Exactly! Oh, look. It's a sign welcoming us to Jamesville. How polite. Although, there's not much here to see, is there? Just woods and more woods."

According to GPS, if she kept going straight, she'd eventually reach the town square and a bit past that would be Hotel Shenanigans, where she had a reservation waiting.

The only problem was that Merry was more interested in exploring the creepy woods.

"What do you think, kittens? Should we just stay on the nice, safe-looking road or go on an adventure? Oh, look! A turn-off. Adventure calls!"

She turned onto the narrow gravel road and followed it through the very spooky-looking woods. Darkness was just beginning to fall, which gave the towering trees an extra dose of sinister gloom. "Exciting, don't you think?"

A few moments later, she came upon another road and without thinking much about it, made the turn and wasn't even surprised when that road ended in a small parking lot.

Right in the middle of the woods.

"Well, this is rather bold for the humans."

A glance in her rearview mirror showed that darkness had fallen just enough so that she really couldn't even see the road she'd followed anymore.

"Creepy road, check. Spooky woods all around, check."

She glanced around, taking note of the only two cars in the lot. "Deserted parking lot, check. Honestly, this is how every horror novel begins, not to mention horror movies. I'm just thrilled." She leaned forward and grabbed several handfuls of chocolate from the dash and the floorboard, stuffing them into the pockets of her hoodie.

She then hopped out of the car, rounded the hood and grinned when she saw the path just beyond the headlights. It was even paved!

She hurried to the passenger side and opened the door.

Two of the kittens were racing around inside the box, chasing each other, pouncing on each other and wrestling one another to the ground.

The other four—no, five—no, six—were piled in a ball in the corner, sound asleep.

Before she could talk herself out of it, Merry reached into the box and scooped one of the wrestling kittens into her arms. Like all his other siblings, he was pitch black. The minute she drew him close, he started batting at her hair. She chuckled, kissed his forehead, then set him back in the box next to his sister, who pounced on him the minute he was within her reach again.

"If I didn't know any better, I'd think you two were hiding a bit of hell-kitten in your genes, which would be wonderful since it's time for an adventure!" She scooped the box into her arms, bumped the car door closed with her hip and started down the path through the woods. "Good thing we got here when we did, kittens. I might not have noticed this path if it were any darker out. Then again, I do have better-than-average eyesight. It's probably the demon in me."

"Mrawr." One of the kittens leapt for freedom and managed to catch Merry's fingers with her claws before sliding back down the side of the box.

Merry let out a hiss and chuckled. "I think I'm going to call you two Spike and Drusilla, in honor of my favorite fictional vampires. You know, just between you and me, I've met a few vampires in my time here on earth—there's an entire coven in Zero, Kansas—but let me tell you, what a letdown! Oh, look, a building." She started walking around it, chatting the entire way.

"The thing is, I guess my expectations were a little different, on account of the books and the movies and all. I expected the vampires to either be, you know, blood-sucking evil demons, or heroic superheroes fighting the evil in our midst. I don't know what that evil would be, mind you—oil companies, people who don't recycle, dentists maybe—but I definitely expected something *more* from the vampires. But you know what, kittens? They were just kind of *boring*."

She finally reached the front of the building and raised an eyebrow at the neon sign above the door.

Shenanigans.

"Well, this is an excellent development. I didn't expect to find a Shenanigans out in the middle of nowhere. Things are looking up, kittens. Zero didn't have any Shenanigans, though they had plenty of paranormals, so that's a little strange. But here in Jamesville, we've already found two! Well, I guess we haven't technically found the hotel yet, but we know it exists!" She pulled open the door and walked inside, "Maybe we'll meet our first serial killer here! That'd be kind of cool, don't you think?"

"Mrawr."

"Oh, but don't worry, kittens. I'll protect you from the big bad wolves. Promise."

"You know, Sam," Pete said, "You should go over and introduce yourself."

"What? Why?"

"You *were* just complaining that your mate hasn't shown up yet," Pete said.

"He's right," Adam said. "What if that's your mate over there? What if she just waltzed into your life, exactly the way you've been hoping, but instead of rushing over there, you're just sitting here on your ass, letting the moment pass you by?"

"Are you serious right now?" Sam demanded. "Did you not hear her talking about serial killers when she walked in? Not to mention the boxful of kittens. Why would you wish that kind of mate on me?"

Max snickered. "Maybe we misheard her."

"Yeah," Cole said. "Maybe she said serial *kittens*, not killers."

"Give me a break," Sam groaned. "There's no such thing as a serial kitten and even if there was, you know that's not what she said."

"Still," Karl said. "This could be your chance, dude."

"You should definitely go over and introduce your-self," Max said.

Sam let out a rumble of annoyance, but the truth was, his wolf had been urging him to go to the woman ever since the door first opened, even before she spoke.

That first gust of wind that had blown through the

bar had carried with it a scent of something purely divine, something that had caught his wolf's attention and set him to howling for more.

The entire situation made Sam appreciate that old saying about being careful what you wished for. He'd made the wish and now he was knee-deep in the consequences.

Grab your copy of *Chocolate Furnanigans* today.

Read on for a bonus excerpt from *Satan's Kitty*.

THAT BYGUL'S LATEST matchmaking efforts resulted in Christmas morning dawning at the Bed & Breakfast in Hell *wasn't* his fault.

He was the top matchmaking cat at Pawsitively Purrfect Matches, for goddess' sake. He was a professional and he didn't make mistakes like that.

He blamed Soraya.

Ever since she saw Jasmine playing with the kittens at the witches' coven house in Zero, Kansas, all Soraya could talk about was matching that little girl with one of the kittens on their caseload *and* matching a mate for her mother, who was both human and single.

Bygul kept reminding Soraya that neither Starlight nor her daughter, Jasmine, were on their caseload, but this didn't matter to Soraya.

"Witches first," Bygul kept saying, "especially after we lost weeks in Jamesville, matching Tempest's sister."

But then, catastrophe struck, no pun intended.

Jasmine wrote a letter to Santa, but before anyone could read it, the letter disappeared and Starlight went into a tizzy, begging her daughter to tell her what she'd asked Santa for.

Jasmine, being the stubborn sort, refused to share. "It's magic, Mom. Magic took the letter to Santa and Santa's gonna take care of everything, so don't worry."

The problem was that Bygul assumed Soraya had stolen the letter, so that she could get details that might help her choose the purrfect kitten for Jasmine.

Soraya assumed Tivali stole the letter for the same reason.

None of them suspected the demon hell-cat, Kyrie.

Unfortunately, being a hell-cat, Kyrie had a lot of magic herself and could pretty much zip around Zero however she pleased.

And apparently, she pleased to steal that letter.

A hell-cat leapt onto Luc's lap, startling him and making him chuckle. "Well, now, when did you get here, Kyrie? Did you get bored in the earth realm already? How's my sweet girl, Tempest, doing?"

Kyrie let out a happy meow and started making biscuits on his legs, causing Luc to yelp and laugh again.

"Okay, okay." He stroked her over and over again until her purr rumbled through the room like a freight train.

Over the next thirty minutes, one by one, Kyrie's kittens, who were no longer kitten-sized, jumped onto Luc's lap to climb all over their mother, batting at her tail and chewing on her ears, until Kyrie lost her patience, slammed a paw on the offending kitten's neck and pinning them down, groomed them to her satisfaction. Eventually, she lifted her paw and the kitten ran away, only to be replaced with another one.

Luc chuckled when he realized that some of the kittens visiting weren't Kyrie's at all. Still she tolerated their play, then groomed each one until the visits finally tapered off.

At that point, Kyrie curled up into a ball and napped for a while.

Of course, during this time, Luc had no choice but to remain motionless, frozen in his chair, a victim of feline purralysis.

Luc felt a terrible mix of both relief and profound

regret, when Kyrie finally stood, stretching leisurely before butting her head against his and jumping down.

"Thanks for visiting, Kyrie," Luc called after her. "We miss you around here."

With a swish of her tail and head held high, Kyrie sauntered from the room.

It was only when she was completely gone that Luc realized she'd left something behind. "What's this?"

An envelope sat on his lap.

It was addressed to Satan Claus, North Pole, from a Jasmine in Zero, Kansas.

Lucifer chuckled. "Haven't received one of these in a long time, now have we, kittens? Ever since the humans automated everything, most of the misspelled letters still make it to good old Mr. Claus. Well, let's see what we can do for Miss Jasmine of Zero, Kansas."

He opened the letter, scanned it and laughed. "Oh, this is going to be sooo much fun."

Start reading *Satan's Kitty* today.

Other Books by Pepper

BLACKTHORN ACADEMY

Monster's Reward

Monster's Madness

MATCHMAKING CATS OF THE GODDESSES

Catnapped

The Real McCat

Unbearably Cute

A Catmas to Remember

This Cat's for You

Santa Kitty

Hocus Purrcus

Abra-CAT-Abra

Tridents & Tails

Her Purrfect Familiar

Chocolate Furnanigans

Satan's Kitty

Valen-Cats

Catanic Rituals

A Beautiful Catship

Going Catty

Grave Cattitude

MURRYSVILLE COALITION

The Crazy Cheetah Lady

One Sad Kitty

SHENANIGANS

Shifter Shenanigans

Witchy Shenanigans

Full Moon Shenanigans

Hotel Shenanigans

Dragon Shenanigans

Undercover Shenanigans

Spooky Shenanigans

Holiday Shenanigans

Valentine Shenanigans

Lucky Shenanigans

STORIES OF THE VEIL

Guardians of the Veil

Astra

Glory

Luna

Zara

Guardians of the Realms

WICKED

No Rest for the Wicked

Wicked Is As Wicked Does

Anthologies & Collections

MATCHMAKING CATS OF THE GODDESSES BUNDLES

The Cat's Meow

Holly Jolly Pawliday

Familiar Meowgic

The Devil's in the Cattails

SHENANIGANS ANTHOLOGIES

Crazed

Amazed

Holidazed

STORIES OF THE VEIL

The Unveiled

The Veiled

COMPLETE SERIES COLLECTIONS

Shenanigans

The Veil

Wicked

About the Author

WWW.PEPPERMCGRAW.COM

PEPPER MCGRAW is a USA Today Bestselling Author of paranormal romance. Her life to date has sadly been paranormal-free, but she expects that will change in time. Until then, she keeps herself busy writing (and reading) paranormal romances.

Pepper loves animals, especially cats, and spends her free time volunteering at local shelters and for Trap-Neuter-Release programs. She's had the supreme honor of winning occasional head butts and meows from the community cats in her neighborhood and has even convinced a few to come inside and adopt her as their own.

amazon.com/author/peppermcgraw

bookbub.com/authors/pepper-mcgraw

facebook.com/ShenanigansSeries

goodreads.com/peppermcgraw

instagram.com/peppermcgraw_author

tiktok.com/@peppermcgraw

x.com/peppermcgraw